FAR OUT
FAIRY TALES

STONE ARCH BOOKS
a capstone imprint

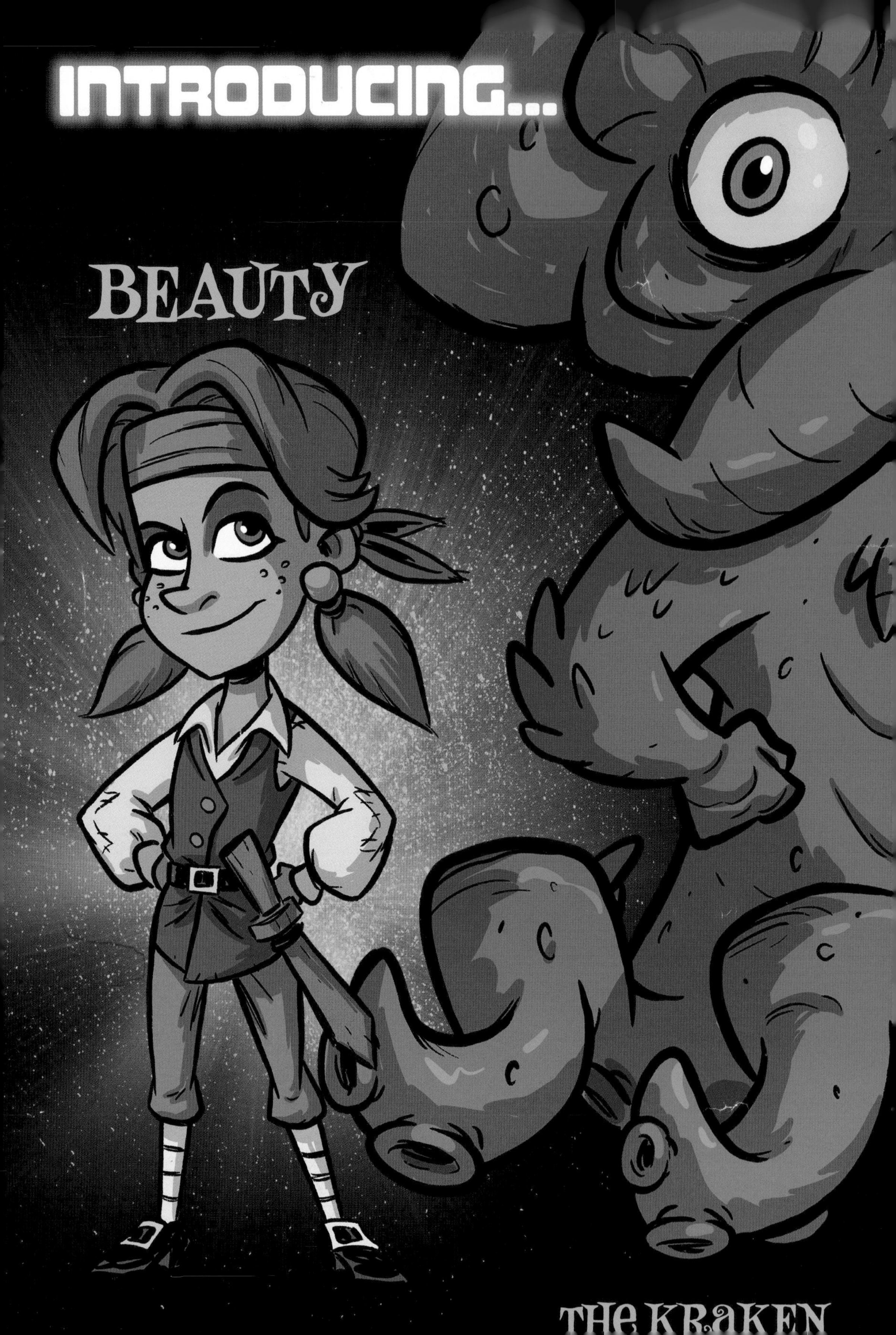
INTRODUCING...
BEAUTY
THE KRAKEN

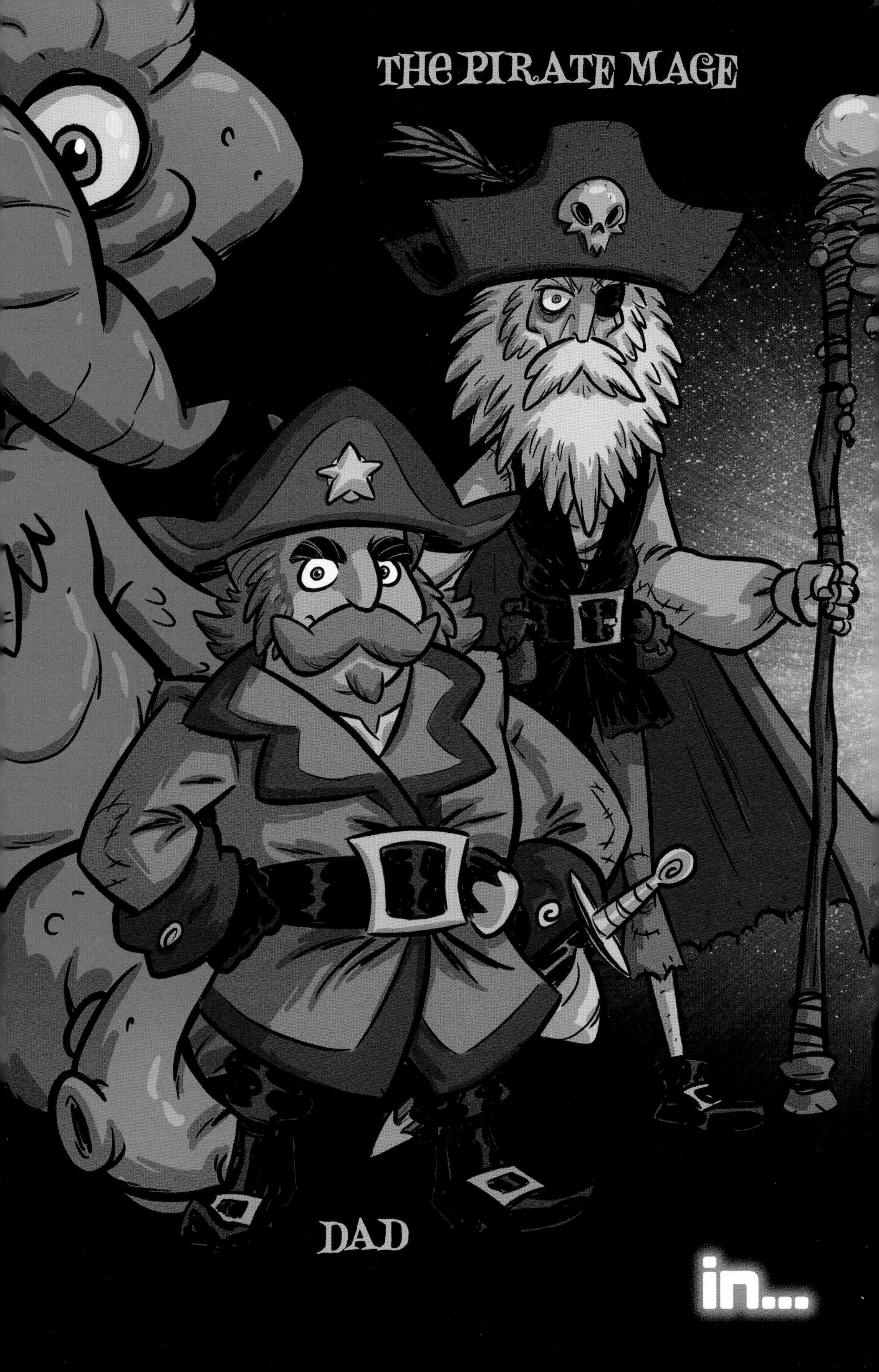
THE PIRATE MAGE
DAD
in...

Far Out Fairy Tales is published by
Stone Arch Books
a Capstone imprint
1710 Roe Crest Drive
North Mankato, Minnesota 56003
www.capstonepub.com

Cataloging-in-Publication Data is
available at the Library of Congress
website.
ISBN: 978-1-4965-8393-2 (hardcover)
ISBN: 978-1-4965-8442-7 (paperback)
ISBN: 978-1-4965-8398-7 (eBook PDF)

Summary: Beauty is sailing the ocean
when pirates attack and her dad is
thrown overboard. Just as he sinks,
something horrible rises—a Kraken!
So Beauty quickly makes a deal to be
the giant squid's prisoner if it rescues
her dad. But as Beauty explores the
island where she's now trapped, the girl
discovers treasure that may hold the key
to saving herself . . . and the sea beast.

Designed by Hilary Wacholz
Edited by Abby Huff
Lettered by Jaymes Reed

Printed and bound in the USA.
PA70

BEAUTY
AND THE DREADED SEA
BEAST

A GRAPHIC NOVEL

BY LOUISE SIMONSON
ILLUSTRATED BY OTIS FRAMPTON

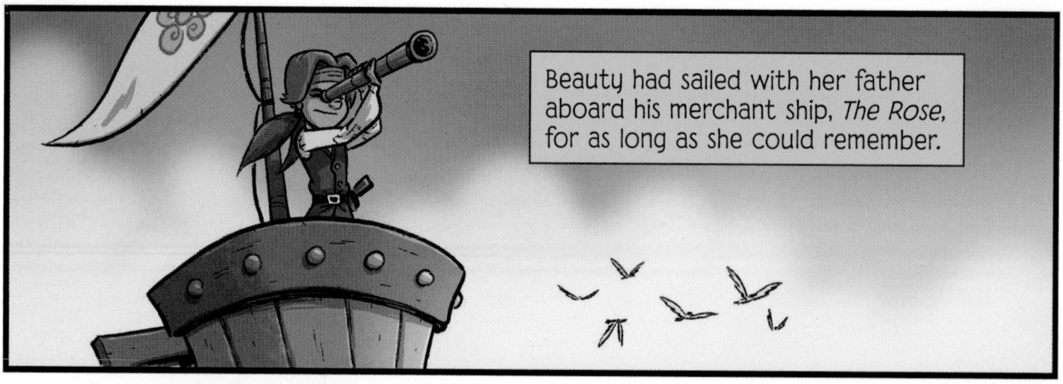
Beauty had sailed with her father aboard his merchant ship, *The Rose*, for as long as she could remember.

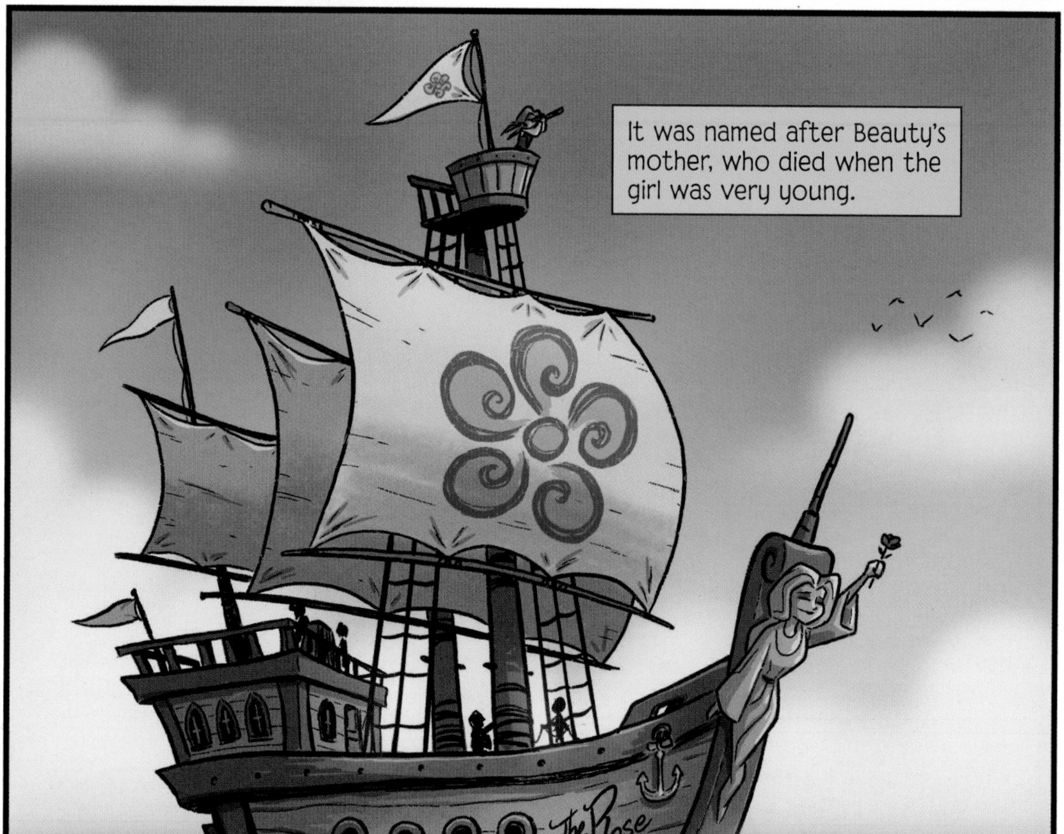
It was named after Beauty's mother, who died when the girl was very young.
The Rose

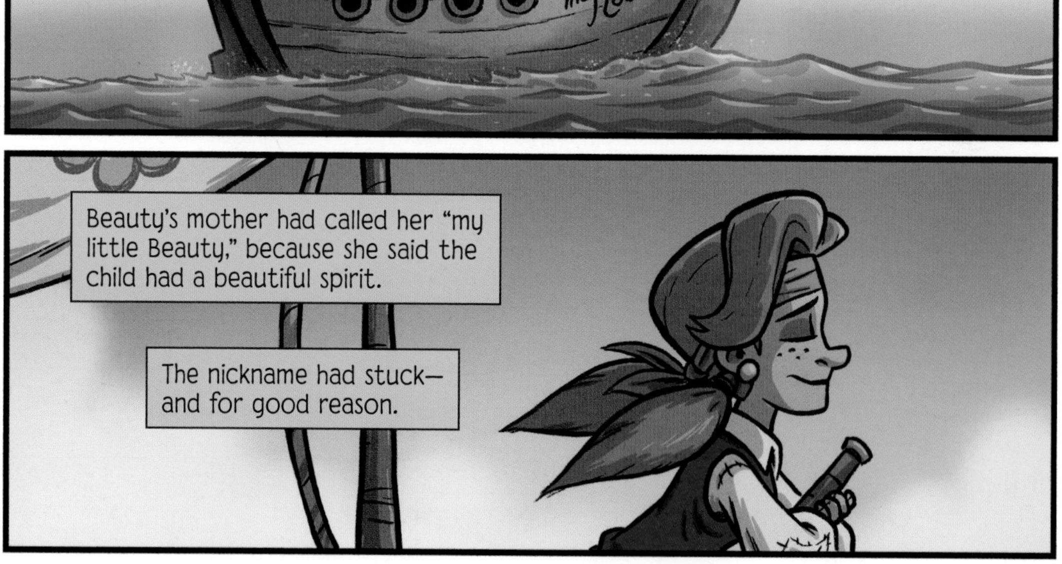
Beauty's mother had called her "my little Beauty," because she said the child had a beautiful spirit.
The nickname had stuck—and for good reason.

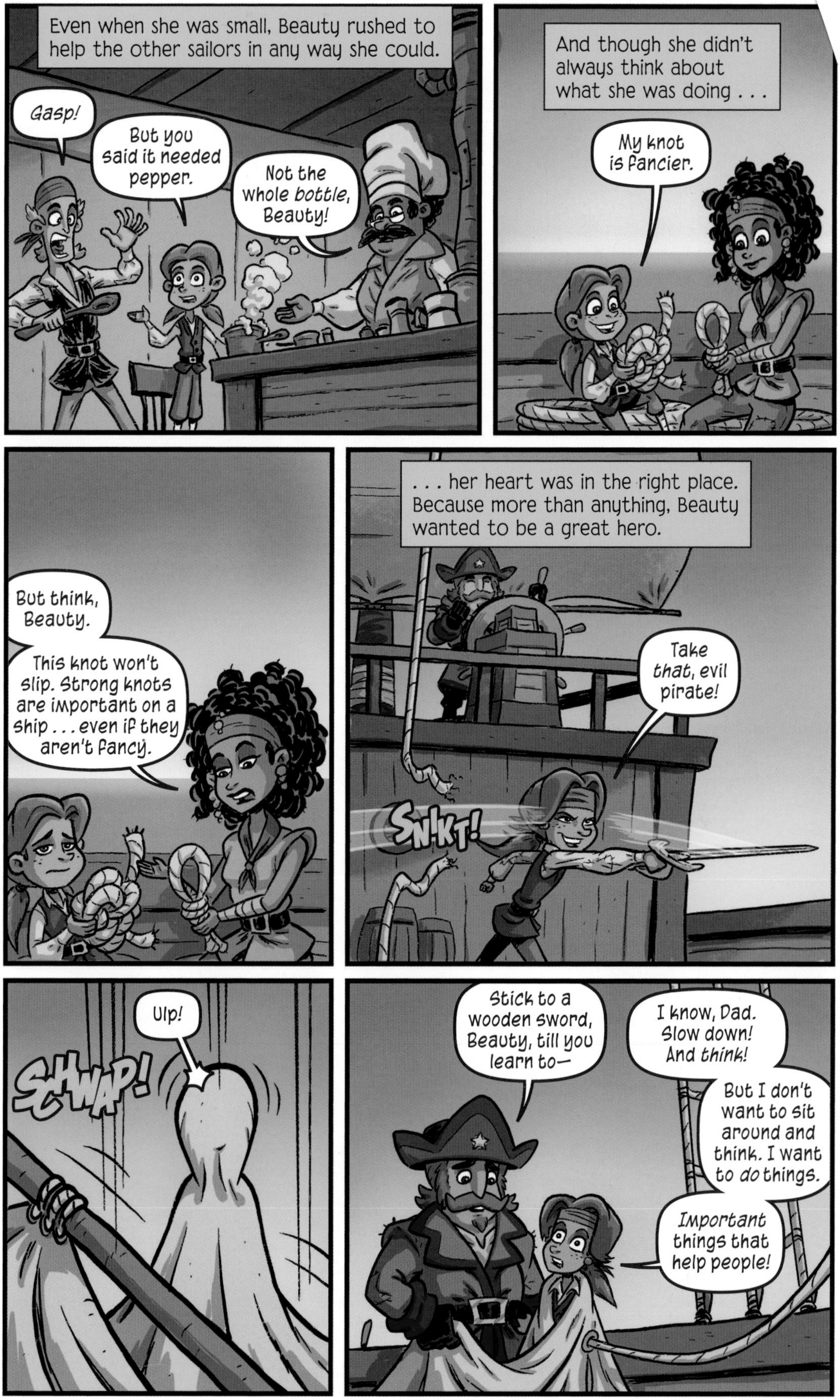
Even when she was small, Beauty rushed to help the other sailors in any way she could.
Gasp!
But you said it needed pepper.
Not the *whole bottle*, Beauty!
And though she didn't always think about what she was doing . . .
My knot is fancier.
But think, Beauty.
This knot won't slip. Strong knots are important on a ship . . . even if they aren't fancy.
. . . her heart was in the right place. Because more than anything, Beauty wanted to be a great hero.
Take *that*, evil pirate!
SNIKT!
Ulp!
SCHWAP!
Stick to a wooden sword, Beauty, till you learn to—
I know, Dad. Slow down! And *think!*
But I don't want to sit around and think. I want to *do* things.
Important things that help people!

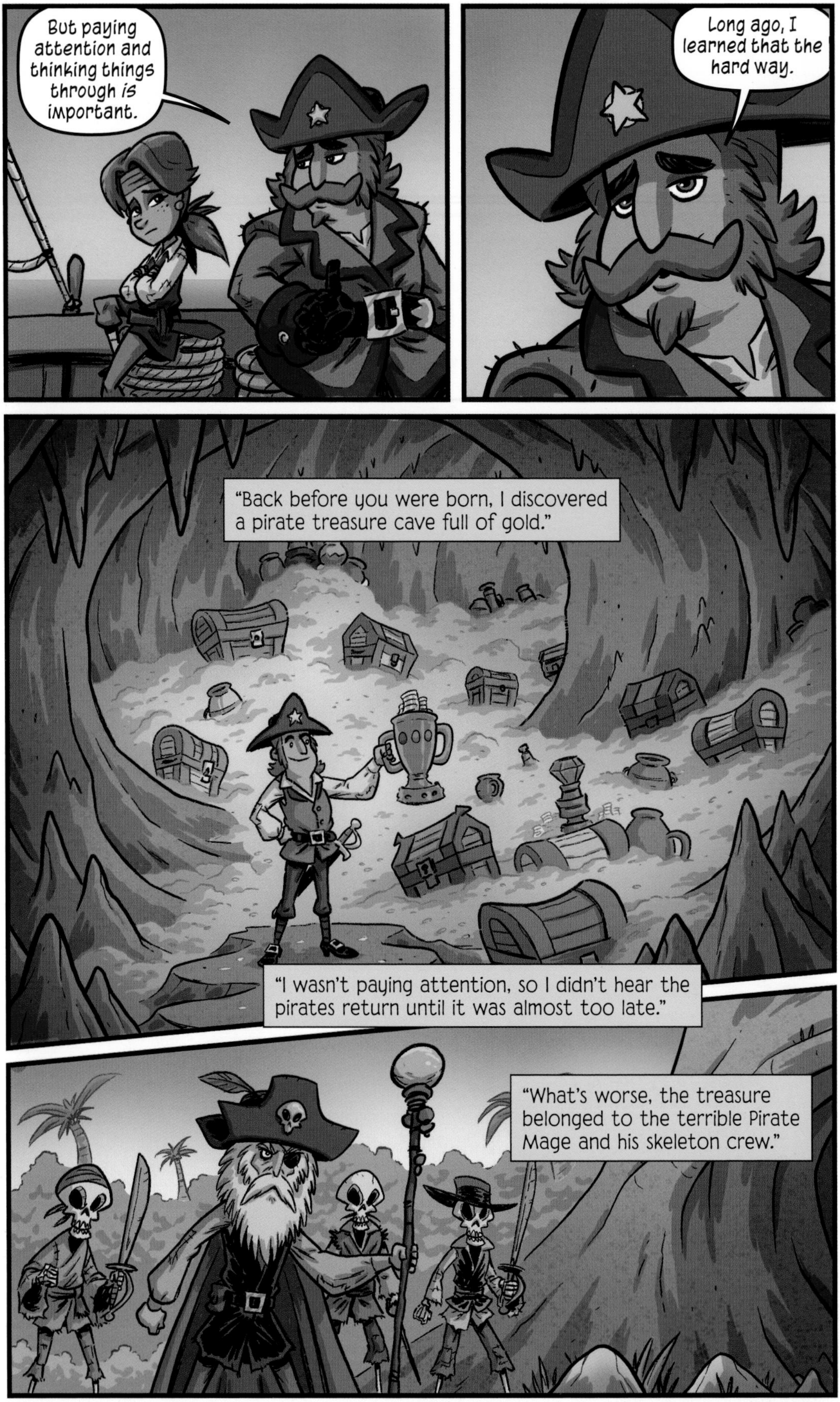
But paying attention and thinking things through *is* important.
Long ago, I learned that the hard way.
"Back before you were born, I discovered a pirate treasure cave full of gold."
"I wasn't paying attention, so I didn't hear the pirates return until it was almost too late."
"What's worse, the treasure belonged to the terrible Pirate Mage and his skeleton crew."

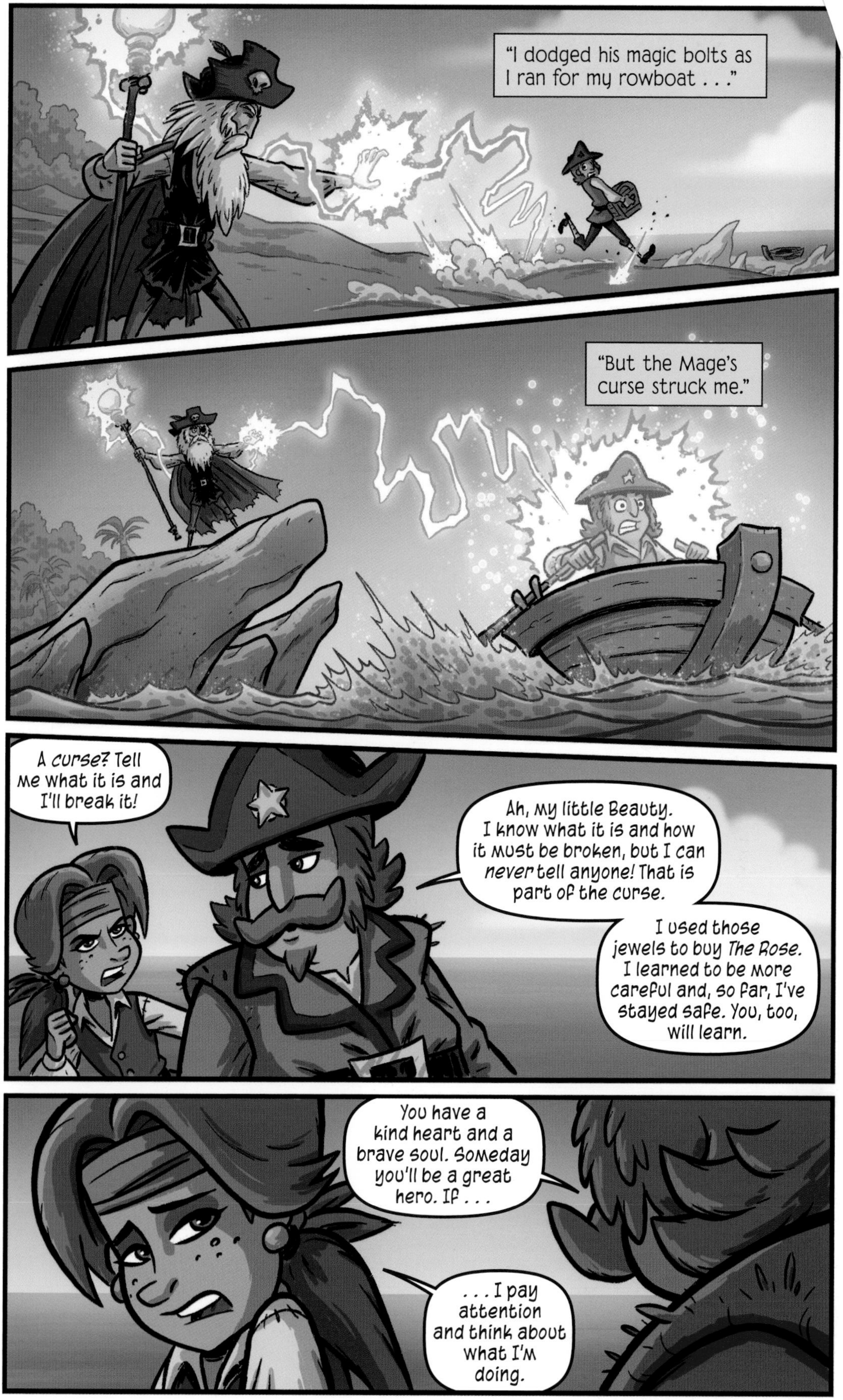

"I dodged his magic bolts as I ran for my rowboat . . ."
"But the Mage's curse struck me."
A *curse*? Tell me what it is and I'll break it!
Ah, my little Beauty. I know what it is and how it must be broken, but I can *never* tell anyone! That is part of the curse.
I used those jewels to buy *The Rose*. I learned to be more careful and, so far, I've stayed safe. You, too, will learn.
You have a kind heart and a brave soul. Someday you'll be a great hero. If . . .
. . . I pay attention and think about what I'm doing.

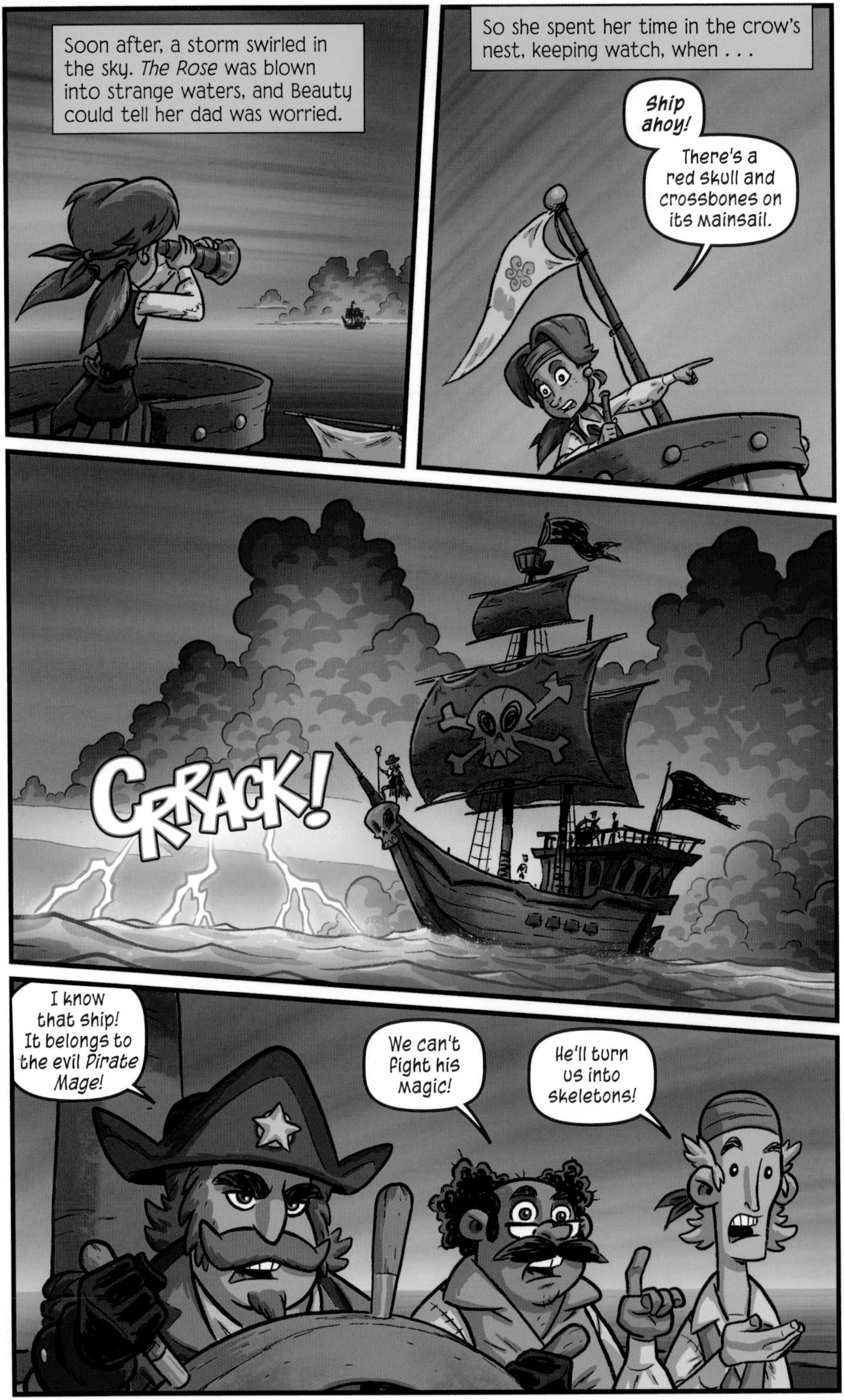
Soon after, a storm swirled in the sky. *The Rose* was blown into strange waters, and Beauty could tell her dad was worried.
So she spent her time in the crow's nest, keeping watch, when . . .
Ship ahoy!
There's a red skull and crossbones on its mainsail.
CRRACK!
I know that ship! It belongs to the evil *Pirate Mage!*
We can't fight his magic!
He'll turn us into skeletons!

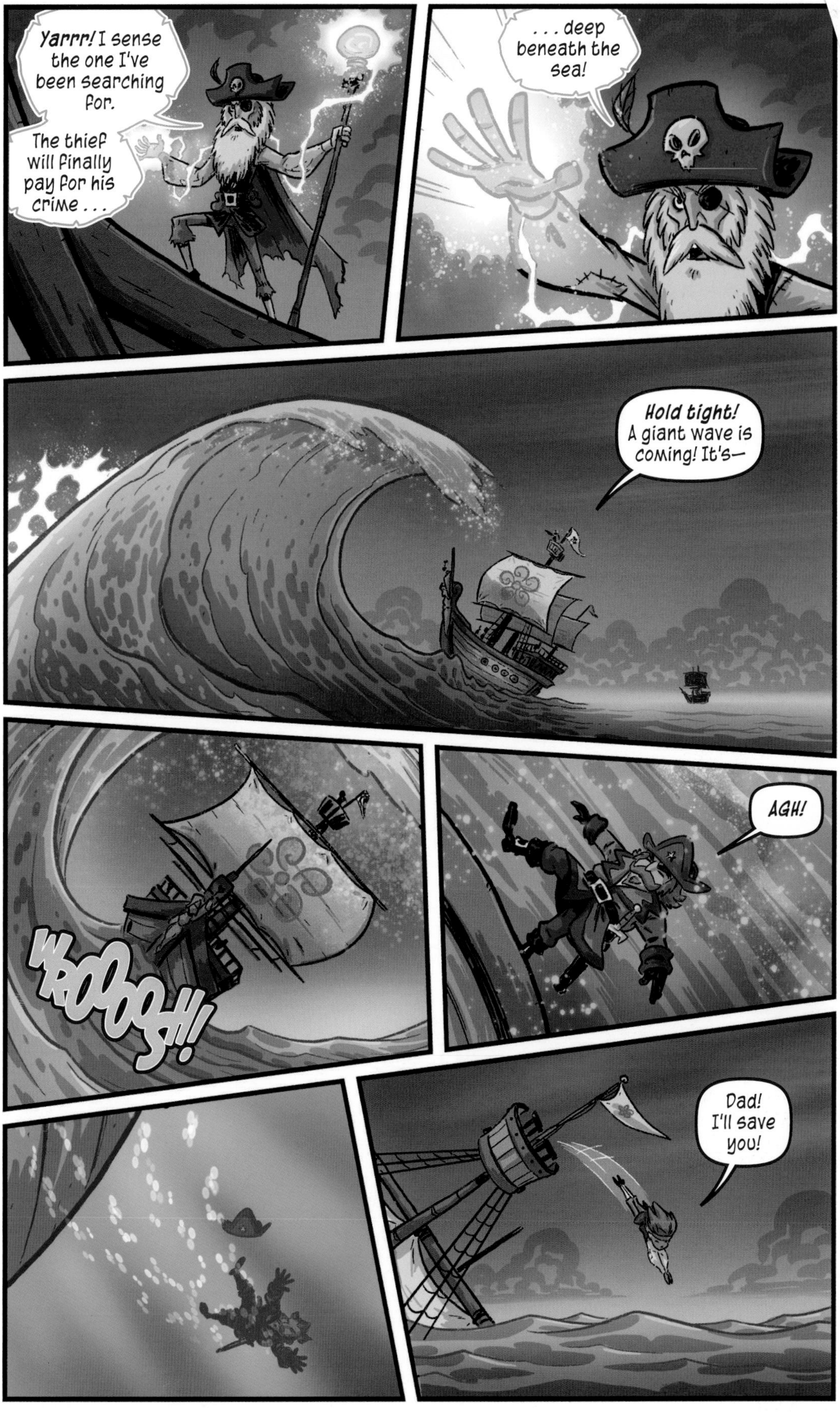
Yarrr! I sense the one I've been searching for.
The thief will finally pay for his crime . . .
. . . deep beneath the sea!
Hold tight! A giant wave is coming! It's—
WROOOSH!!
AGH!
Dad! I'll save you!

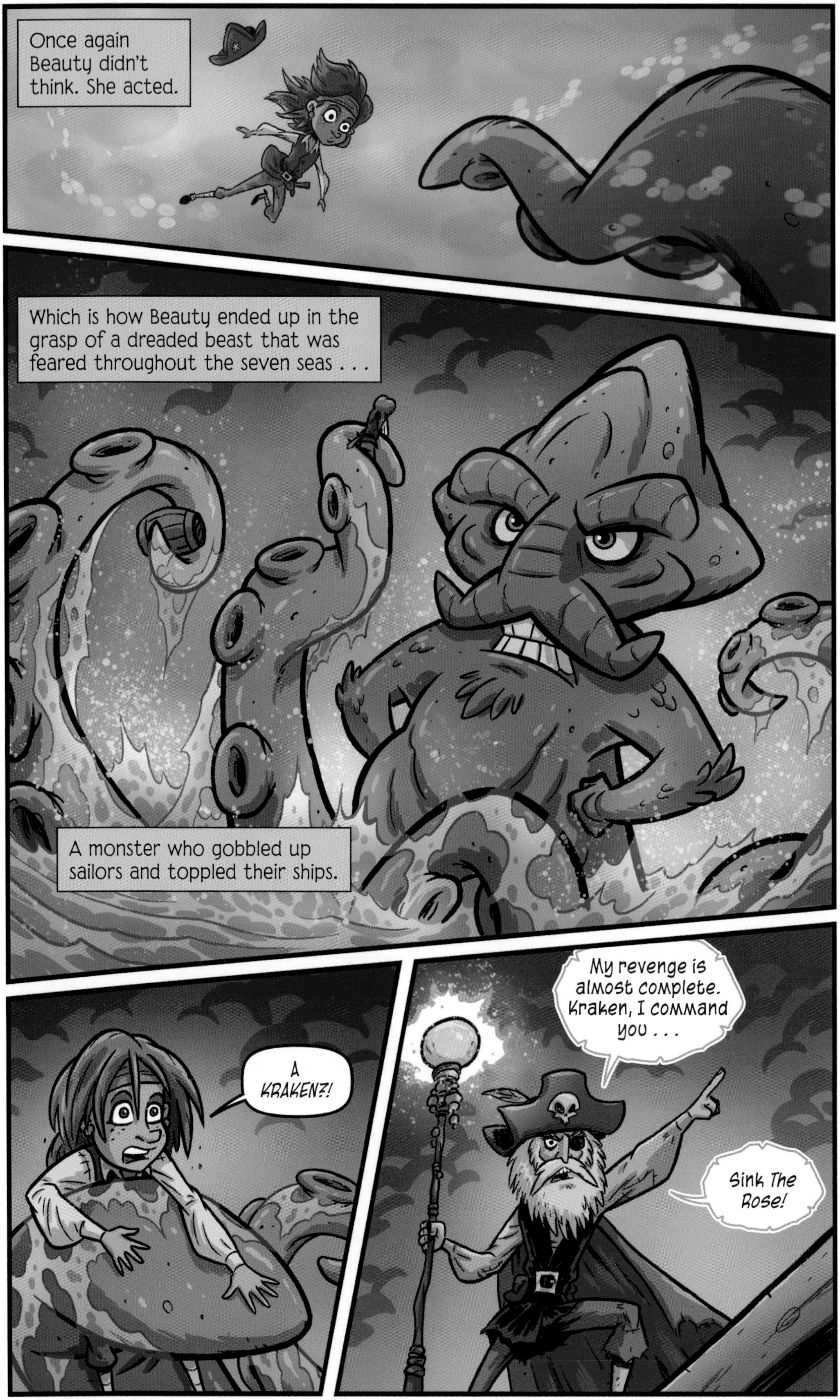
Once again Beauty didn't think. She acted.
Which is how Beauty ended up in the grasp of a dreaded beast that was feared throughout the seven seas . . .
A monster who gobbled up sailors and toppled their ships.
A KRAKEN?!
My revenge is almost complete. Kraken, I command you . . .
Sink The Rose!

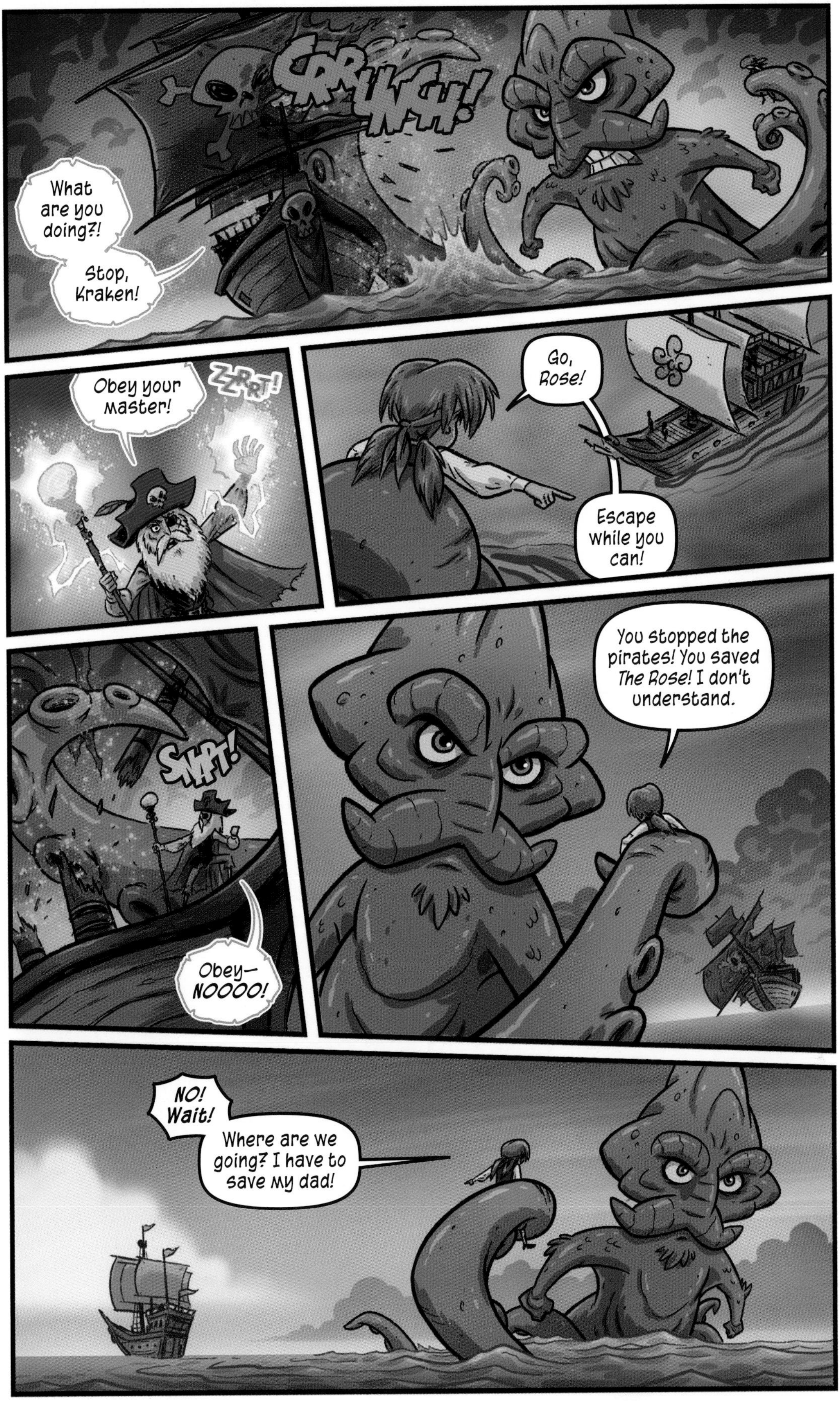
CRRUNCH!
What are you doing?!
Stop, Kraken!
Obey your master!
ZZRRT!
Go, Rose!
Escape while you can!
SNAPT!
Obey—NOOOO!
You stopped the pirates! You saved The Rose! I don't understand.
NO! Wait!
Where are we going? I have to save my dad!

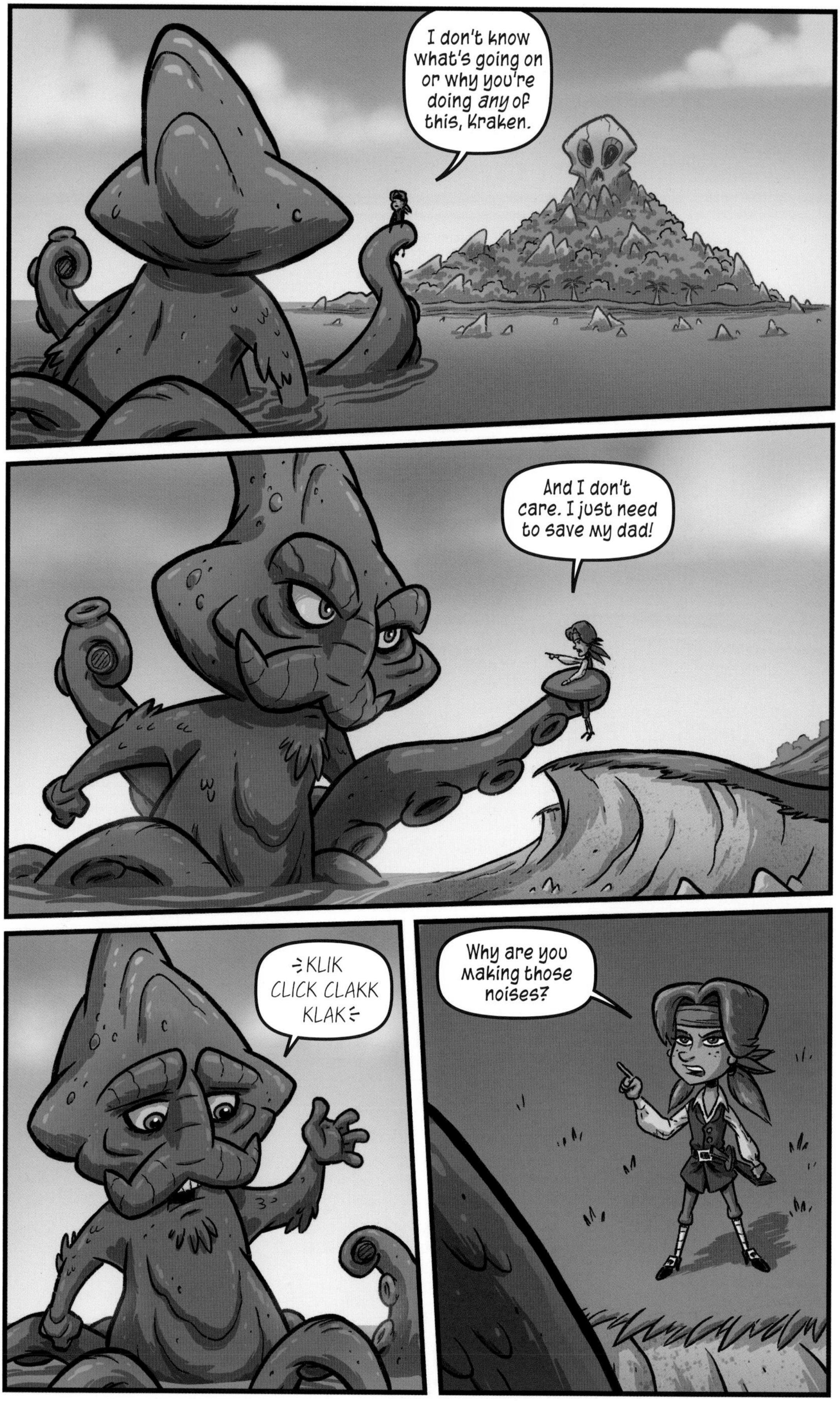
I don't know what's going on or why you're doing *any* of this, Kraken.
And I don't care. I just need to save my dad!
KLIK CLICK CLAKK KLAK
Why are you making those noises?

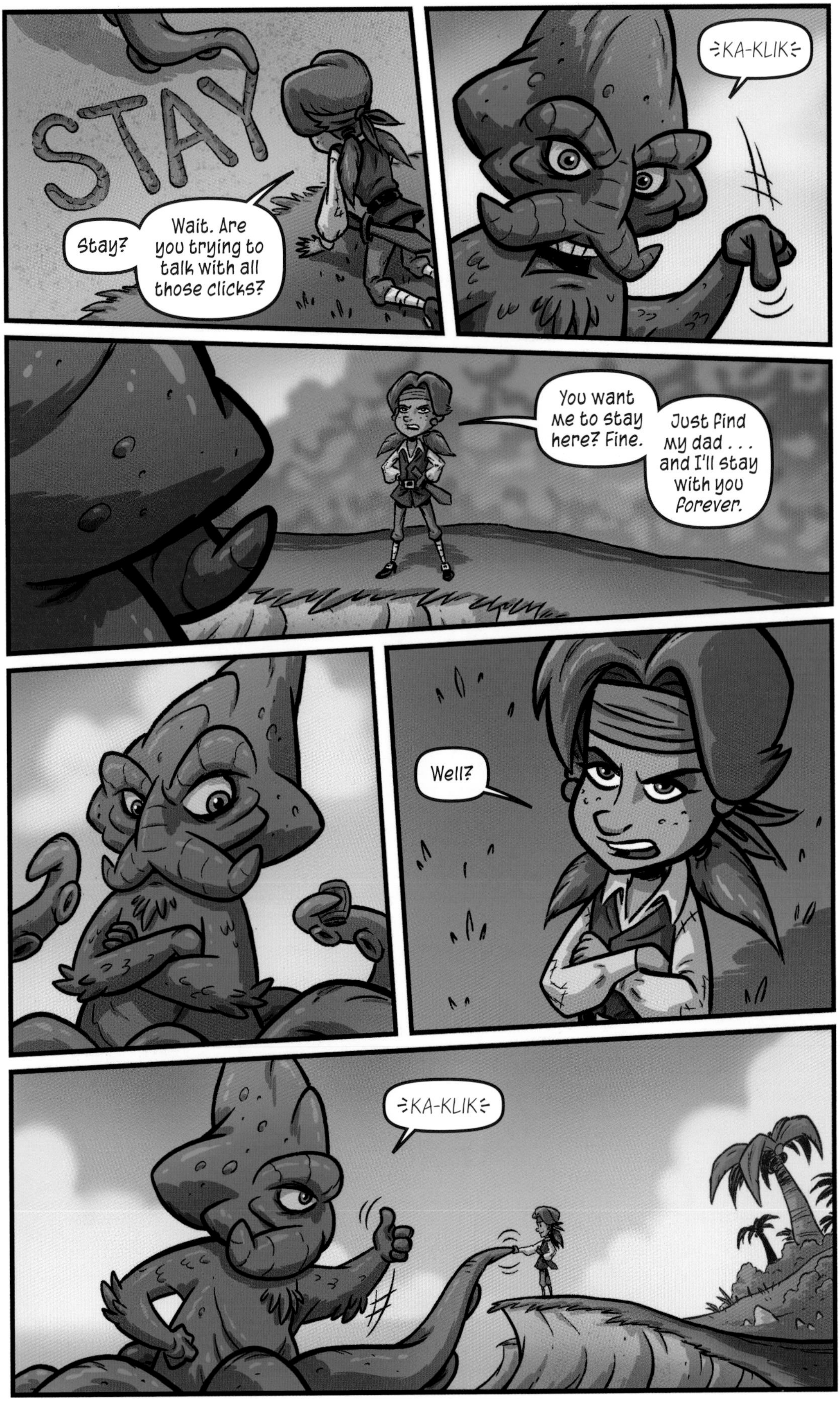
STAY
Stay?
Wait. Are you trying to talk with all those clicks?
KA-KLIK
You want me to stay here? Fine.
Just find my dad . . . and I'll stay with you *forever.*
Well?
KA-KLIK

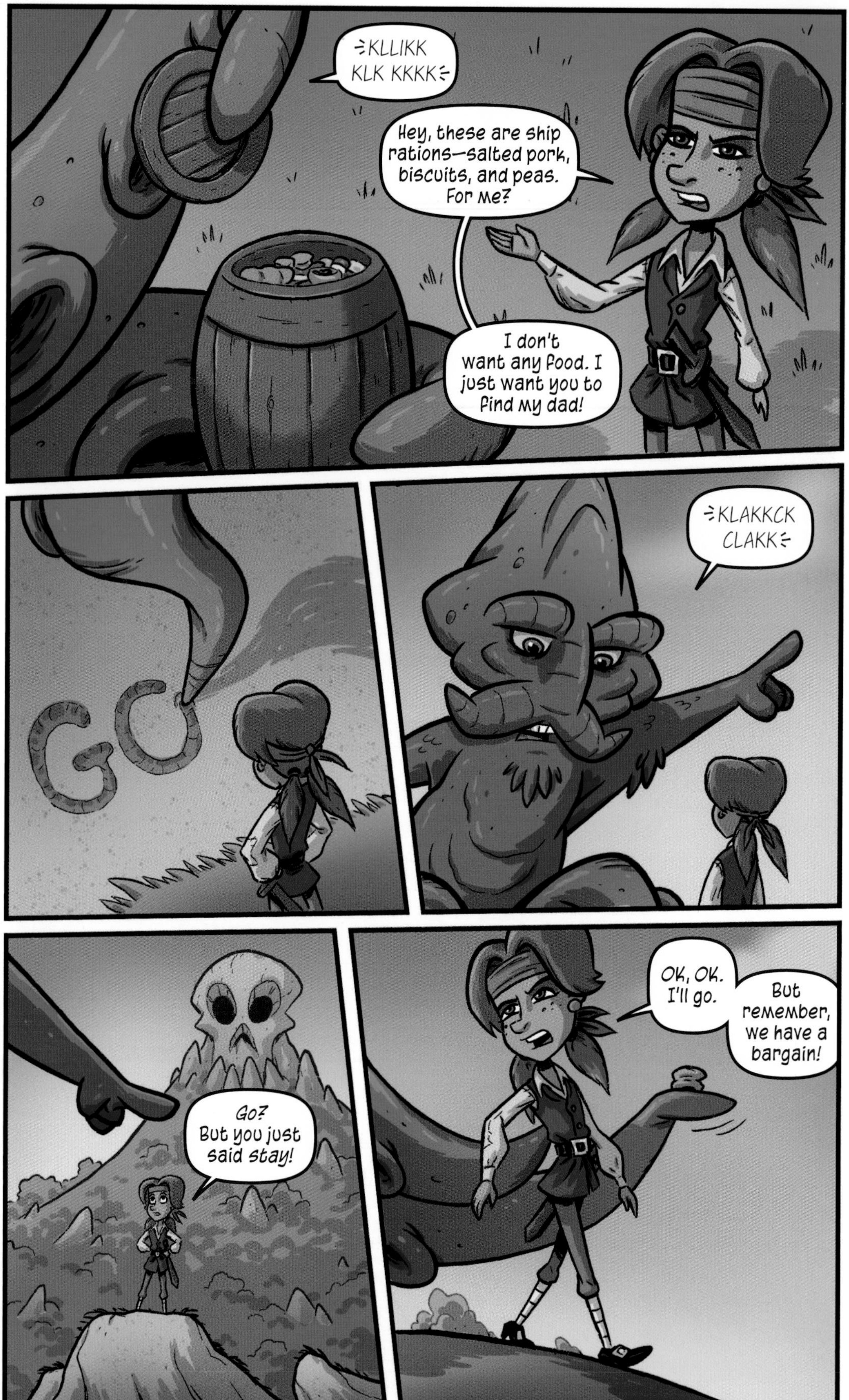
KLLIKK KLK KKKK
Hey, these are ship rations—salted pork, biscuits, and peas. For me?
I don't want any food. I just want you to find my dad!
GO
KLAKKCK CLAKK
Go? But you just said stay!
OK, OK. I'll go.
But remember, we have a bargain!

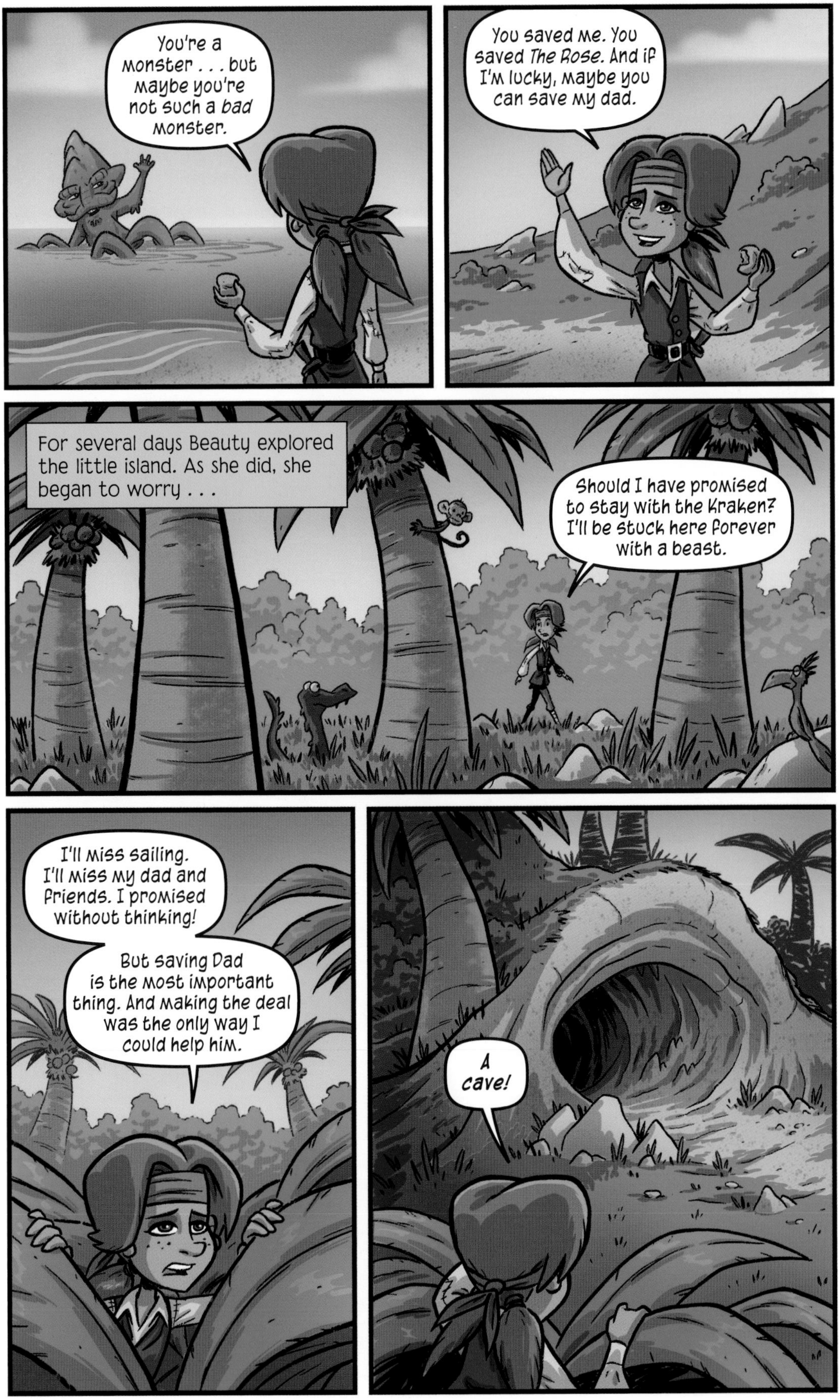
You're a monster . . . but maybe you're not such a *bad* monster.
You saved me. You saved *The Rose*. And if I'm lucky, maybe you can save my dad.
For several days Beauty explored the little island. As she did, she began to worry . . .
Should I have promised to stay with the Kraken? I'll be stuck here forever with a beast.
I'll miss sailing. I'll miss my dad and friends. I promised without thinking!
But saving Dad is the most important thing. And making the deal was the only way I could help him.
A cave!

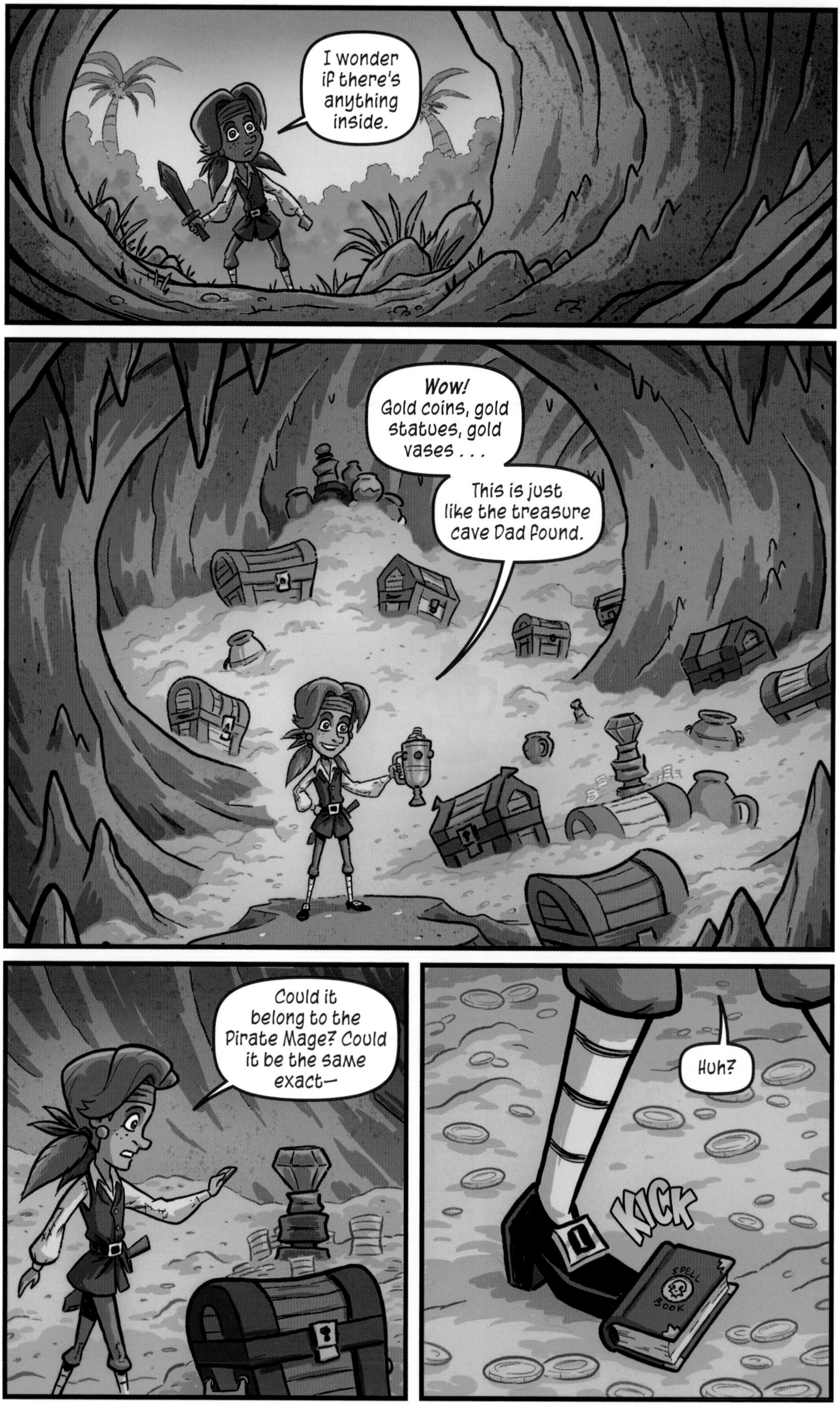
I wonder if there's anything inside.
Wow! Gold coins, gold statues, gold vases . . .
This is just like the treasure cave Dad found.
Could it belong to the Pirate Mage? Could it be the same exact—
Huh?
KICK
SPELL BOOK

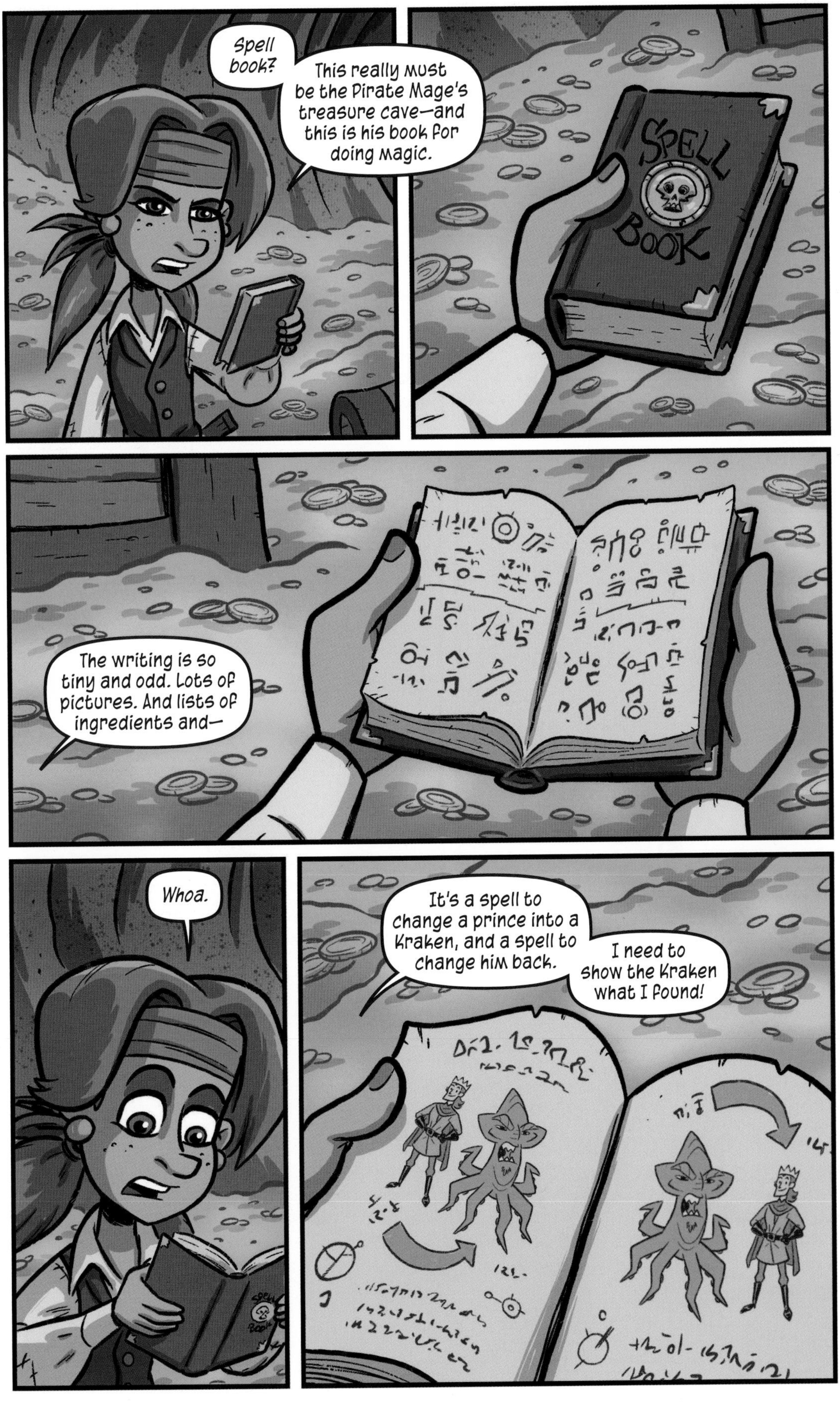
Spell book?
This really must be the Pirate Mage's treasure cave—and this is his book for doing magic.
SPELL BOOK
The writing is so tiny and odd. Lots of pictures. And lists of ingredients and—
Whoa.
It's a spell to change a prince into a Kraken, and a spell to change him back.
I need to show the Kraken what I found!

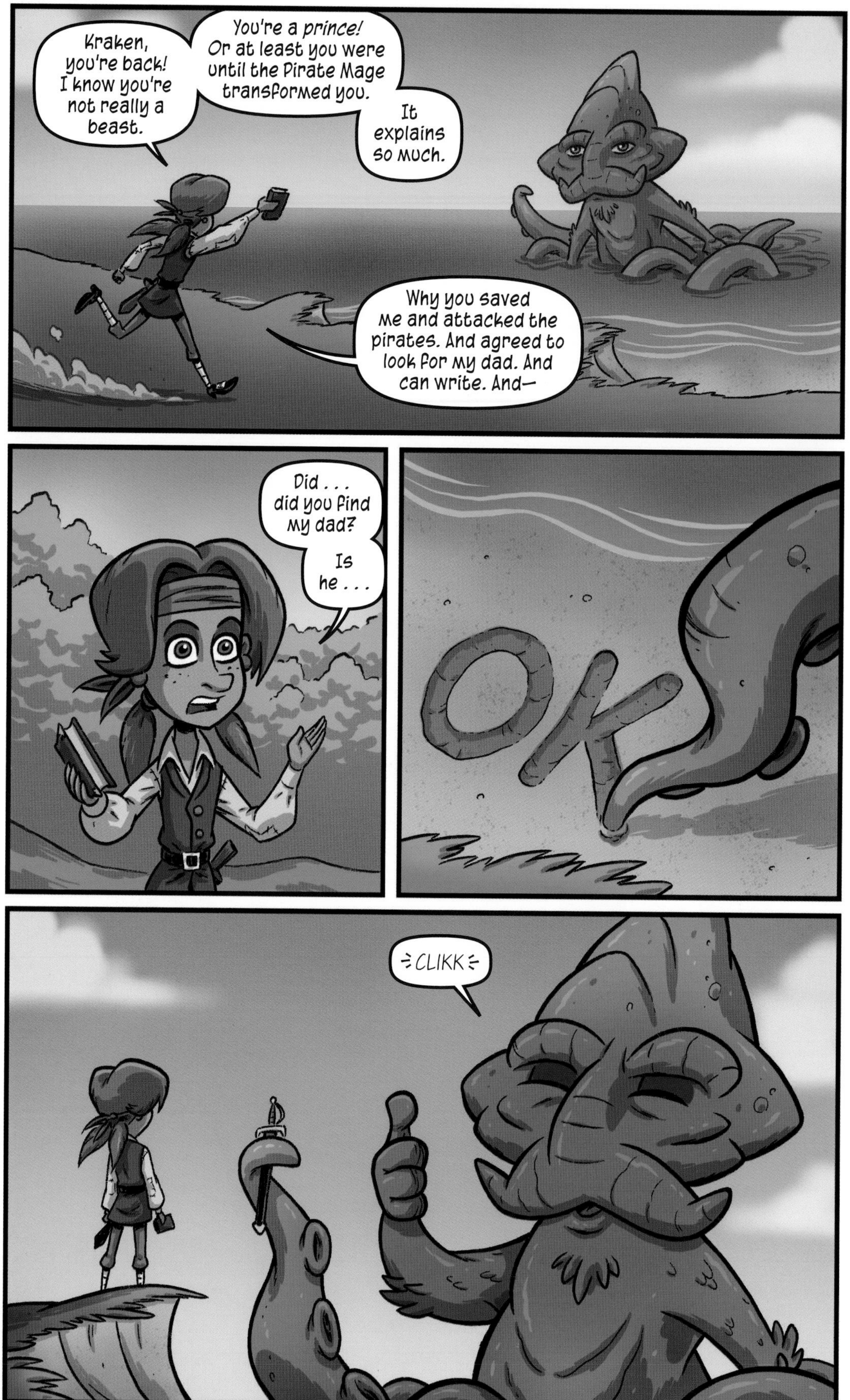
Kraken, you're back! I know you're not really a beast.
You're a *prince!* Or at least you were until the Pirate Mage transformed you.
It explains so much.
Why you saved me and attacked the pirates. And agreed to look for my dad. And can write. And—
Did . . . did you find my dad?
Is he . . .
OK
CLIKK

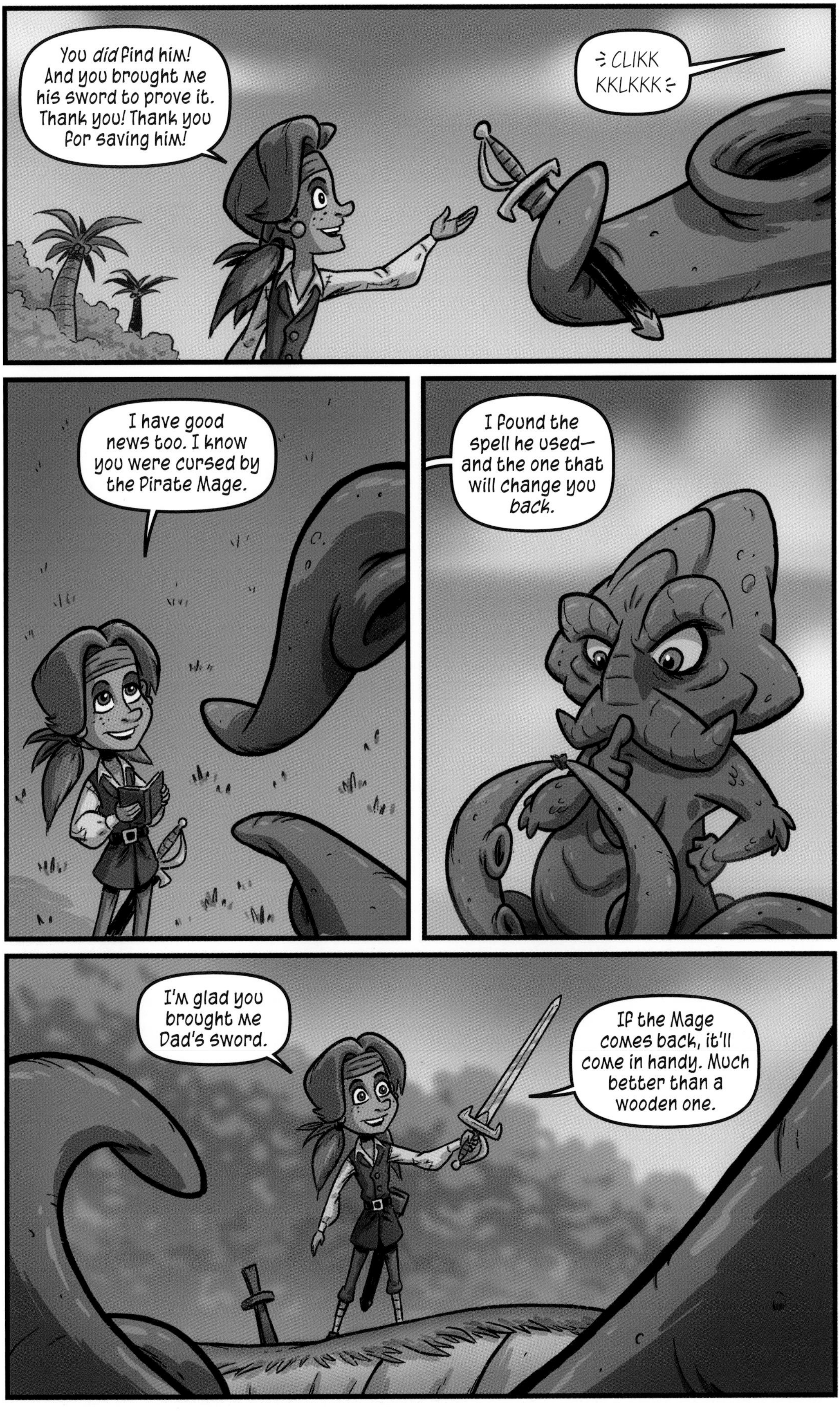
You *did* find him! And you brought me his sword to prove it. Thank you! Thank you for saving him!
CLIKK KKLKKK
I have good news too. I know you were cursed by the Pirate Mage.
I found the spell he used—and the one that will change you back.
I'm glad you brought me Dad's sword.
If the Mage comes back, it'll come in handy. Much better than a wooden one.

Beauty and the Kraken spent hours figuring out the strange writing.

Then they made a list of ingredients they would need to break the curse.

Tooth of a Viper Fish
Sand Dollar
Bottle With a Message Inside
Glass Sponge

Skele... Sorcerer... eel
Venus ...p A...

Day after day, the Kraken swam off. And day after day, he returned with another item on the list.

The skeleton of a sorcerer eel! Excellent!

22

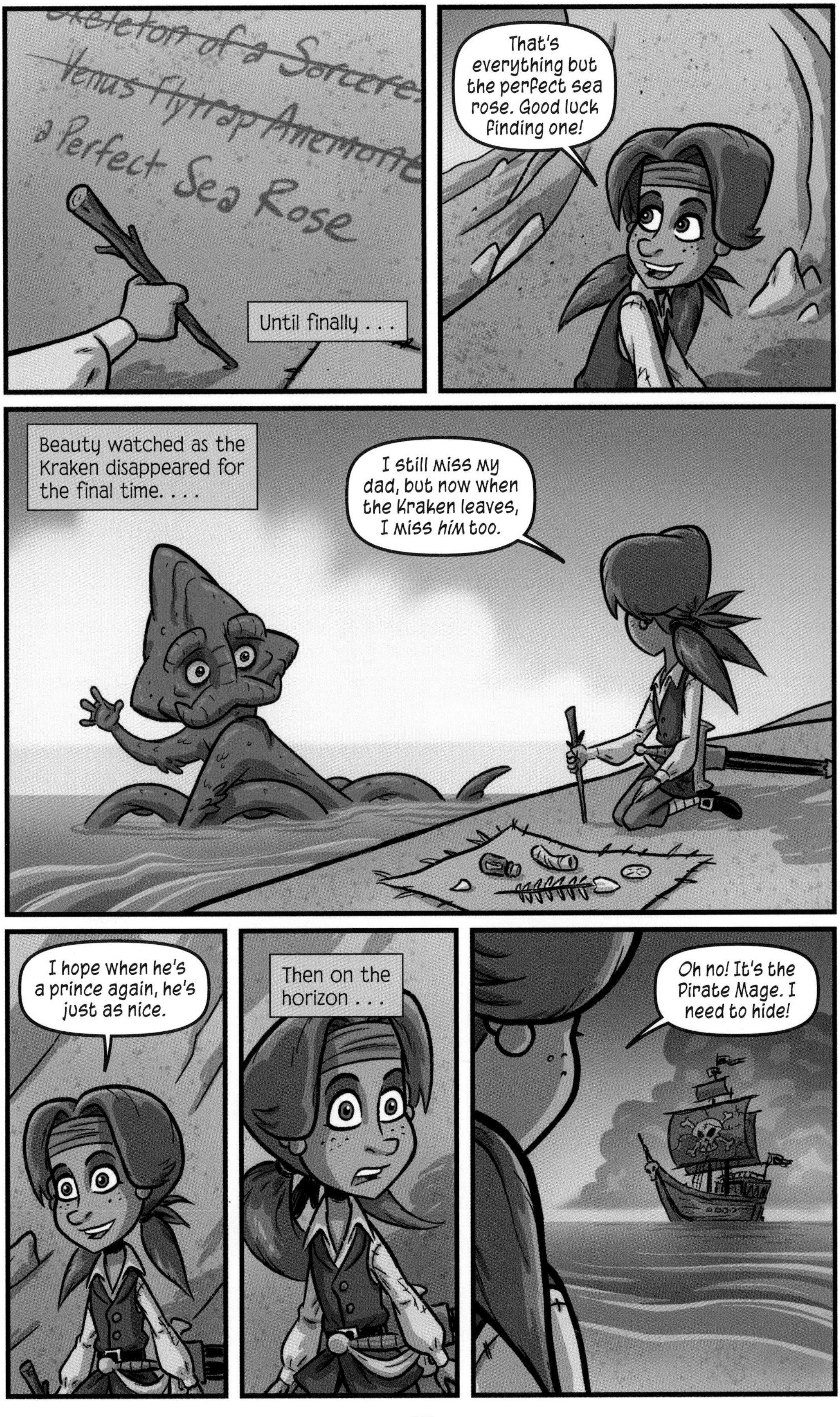
~~keleton of a Sorcere~~
~~Venus Flytrap Anemone~~
a Perfect Sea Rose
Until finally . . .
That's everything but the perfect sea rose. Good luck finding one!
Beauty watched as the Kraken disappeared for the final time. . . .
I still miss my dad, but now when the Kraken leaves, I miss *him* too.
I hope when he's a prince again, he's just as nice.
Then on the horizon . . .
Oh no! It's the Pirate Mage. I need to hide!

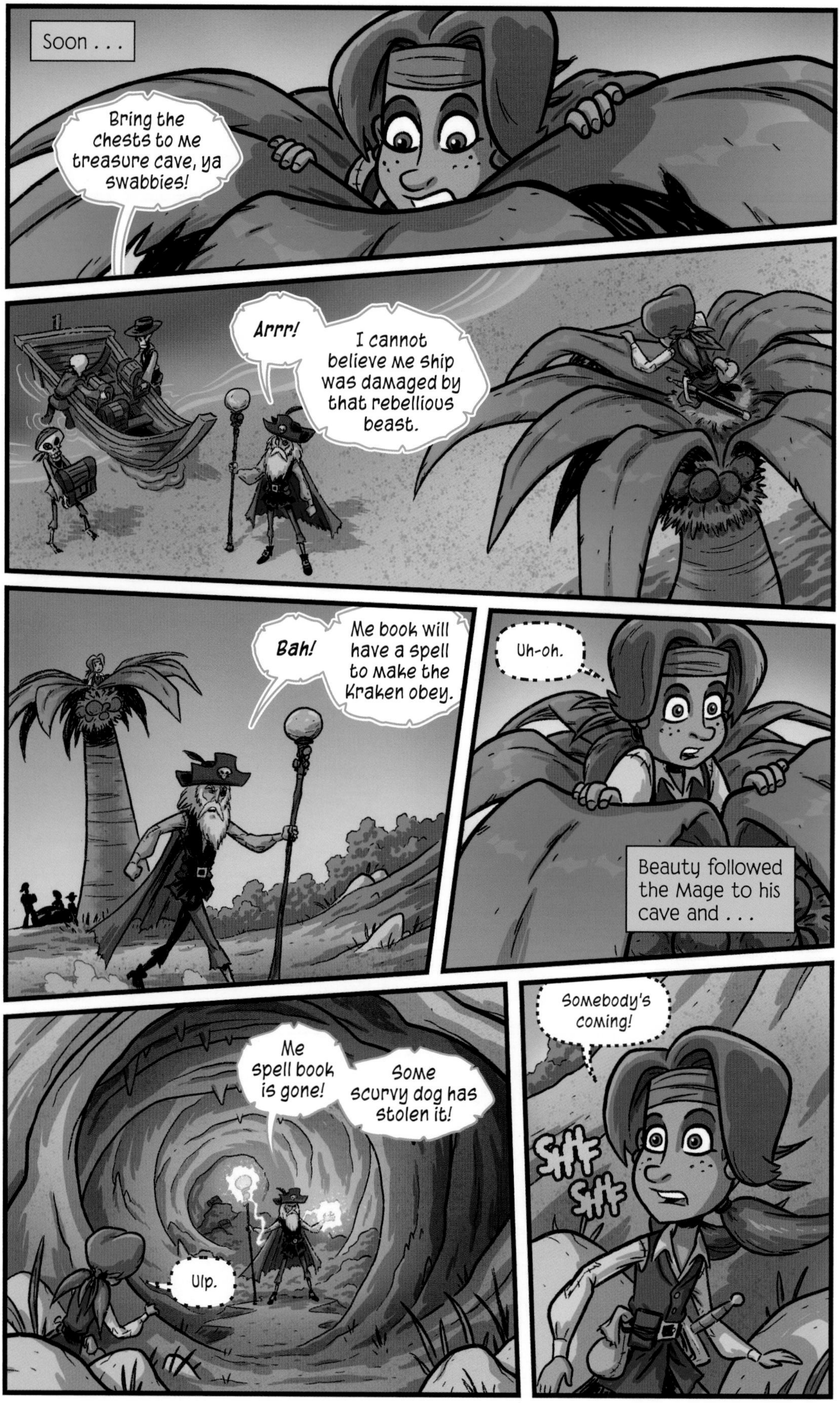
Soon . . .
Bring the chests to me treasure cave, ya swabbies!
Arrr!
I cannot believe me ship was damaged by that rebellious beast.
Bah!
Me book will have a spell to make the Kraken obey.
Uh-oh.
Beauty followed the Mage to his cave and . . .
Me spell book is gone!
Some scurvy dog has stolen it!
Ulp.
Somebody's coming!
SHF
SHF

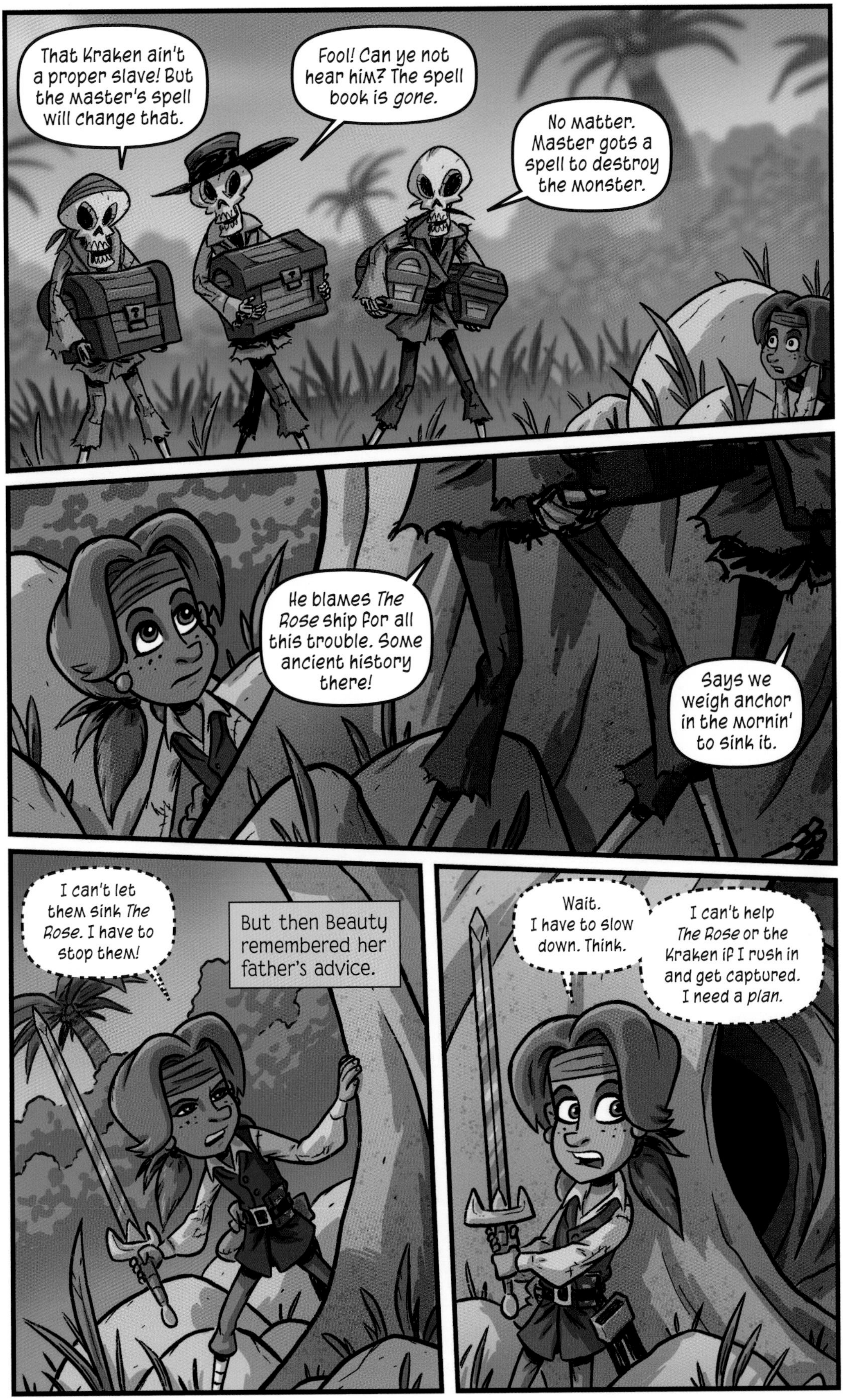

That Kraken ain't a proper slave! But the master's spell will change that.
Fool! Can ye not hear him? The spell book is *gone.*
No matter. Master gots a spell to destroy the monster.
He blames *The Rose* ship for all this trouble. Some ancient history there!
Says we weigh anchor in the mornin' to sink it.
I can't let them sink *The Rose.* I have to stop them!
But then Beauty remembered her father's advice.
Wait. I have to slow down. Think.
I can't help *The Rose* or the Kraken if I rush in and get captured. I need a *plan.*

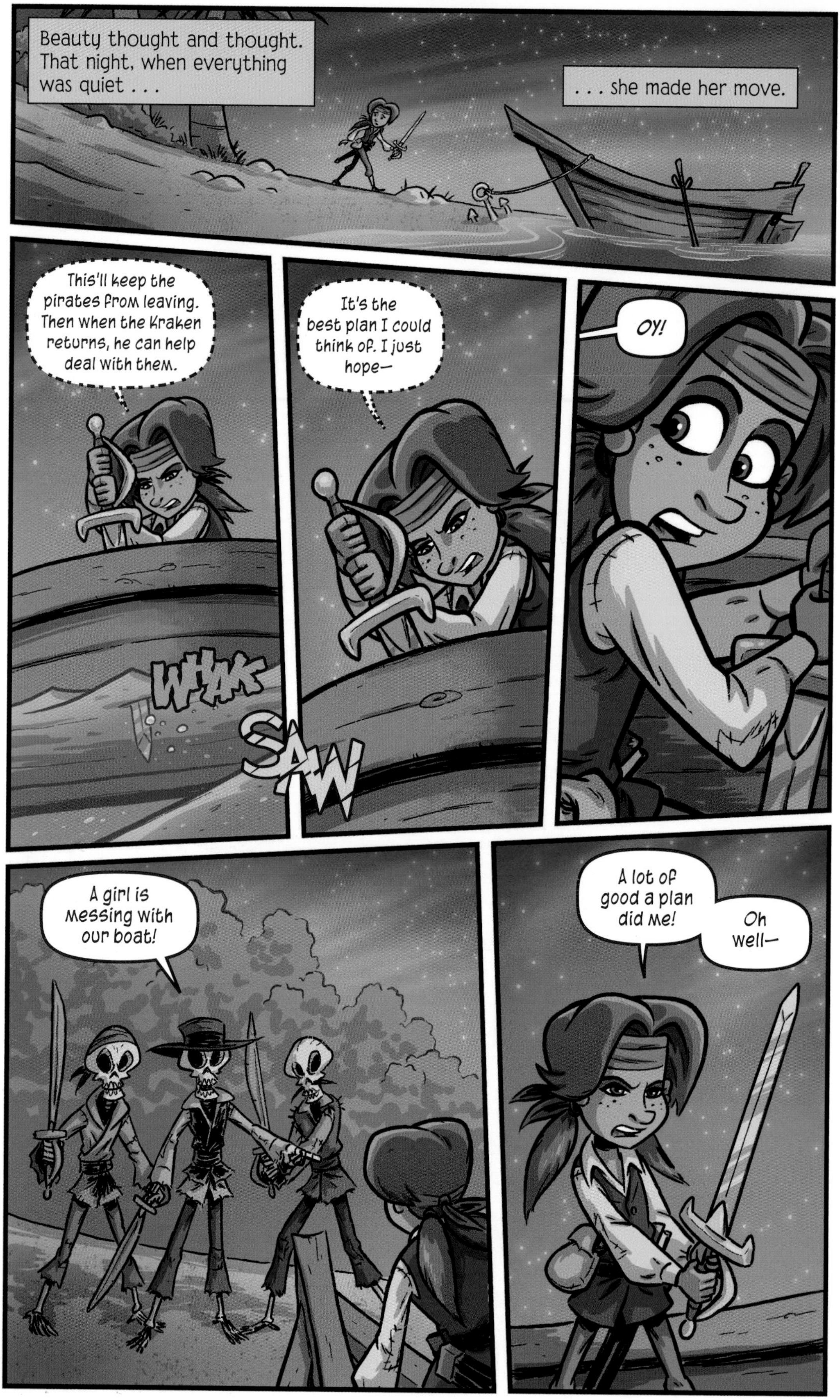

Beauty thought and thought. That night, when everything was quiet . . .
. . . she made her move.
This'll keep the pirates from leaving. Then when the Kraken returns, he can help deal with them.
WHAK
SAW
It's the best plan I could think of. I just hope—
OY!
A girl is messing with our boat!
A lot of good a plan did me!
Oh well—

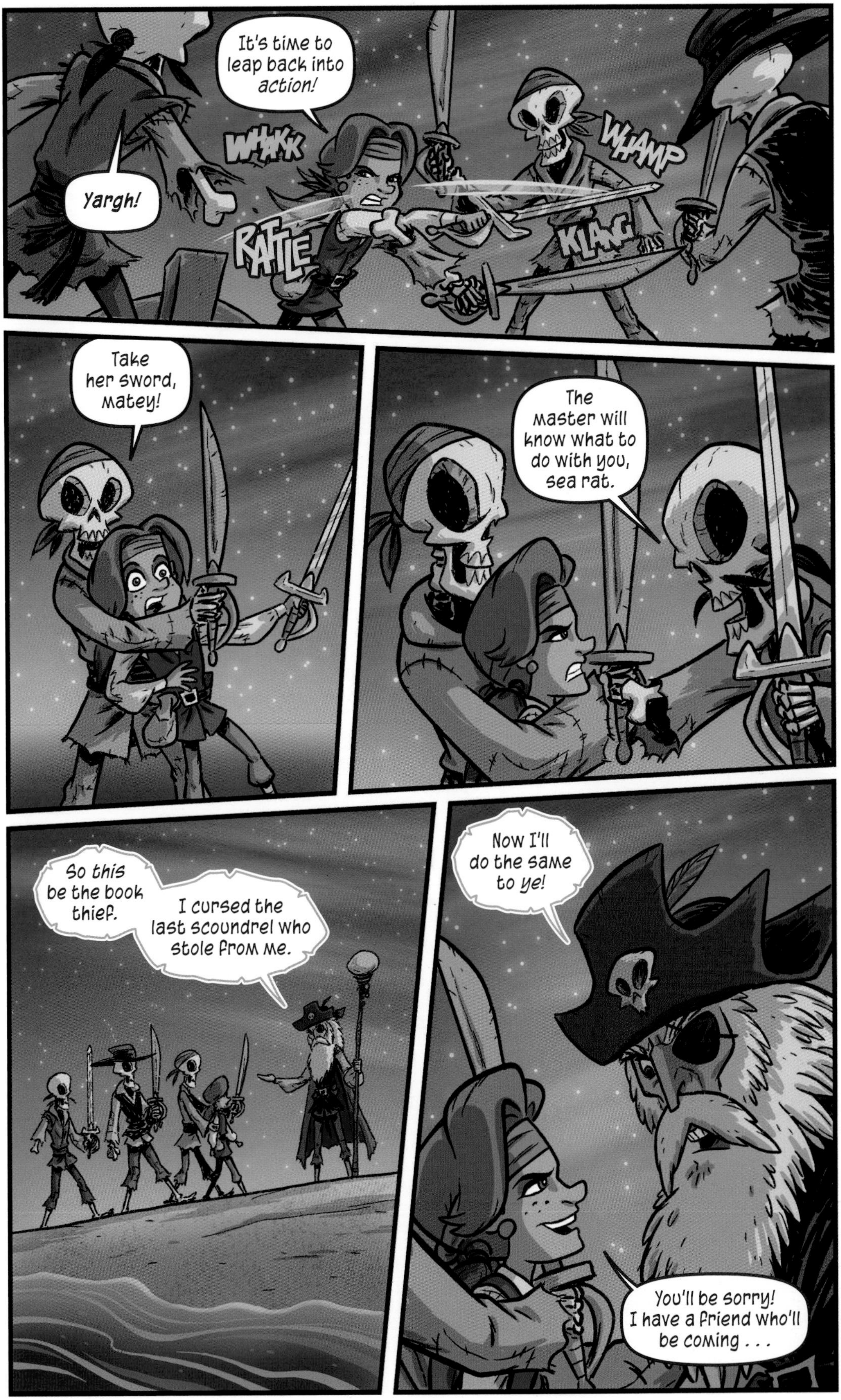
It's time to leap back into action!
Yargh!
WHAKK
WHAMP
RATTLE
KLANG
Take her sword, Matey!
The master will know what to do with you, sea rat.
So this be the book thief.
I cursed the last scoundrel who stole from me.
Now I'll do the same to ye!
You'll be sorry! I have a friend who'll be coming . . .

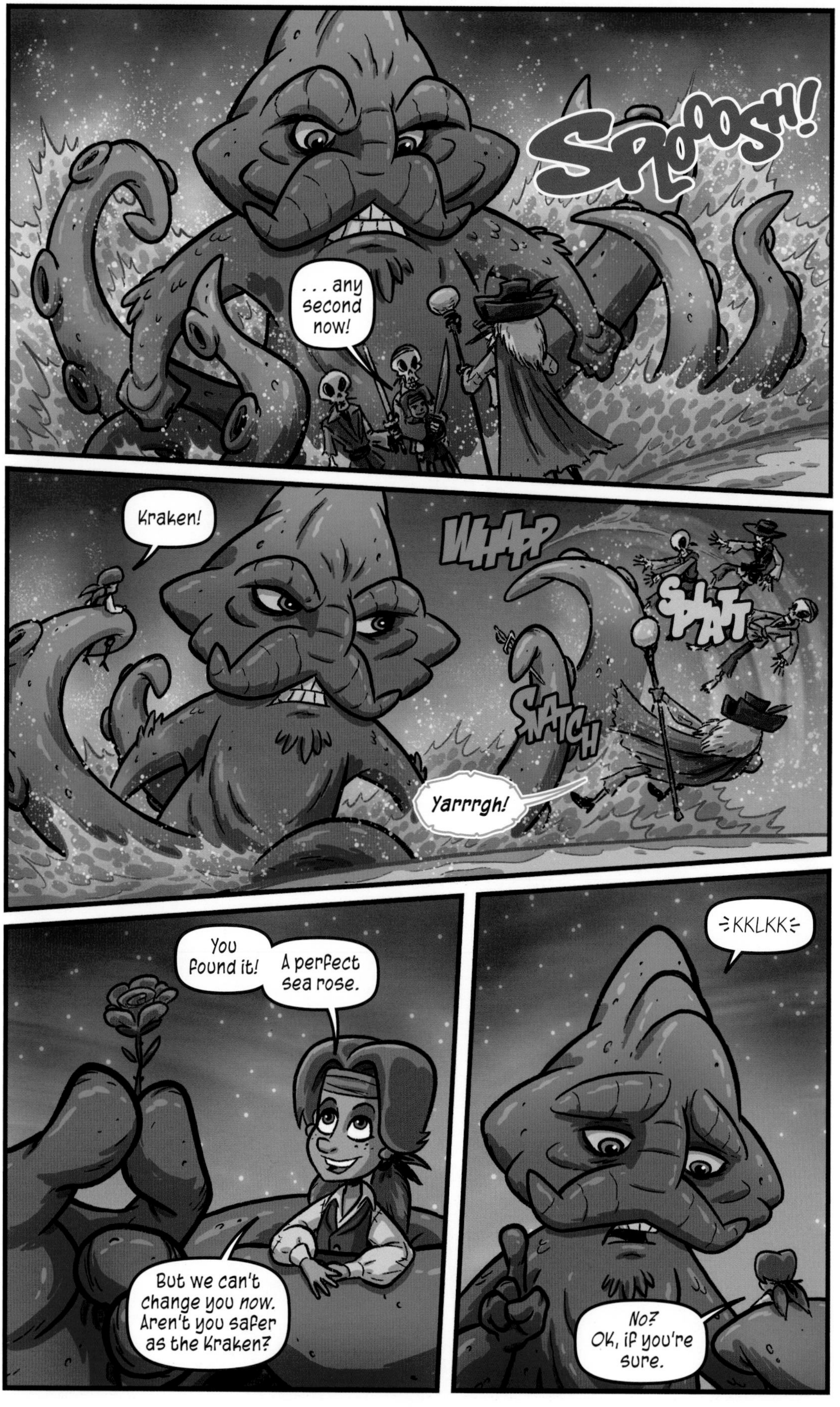
SPLOOOSH!
. . . any second now!
Kraken!
WHAPP
SPLATT
SNATCH
Yarrrgh!
You found it!
A perfect sea rose.
But we can't change you now. Aren't you safer as the Kraken?
KKLKK
No? OK, if you're sure.

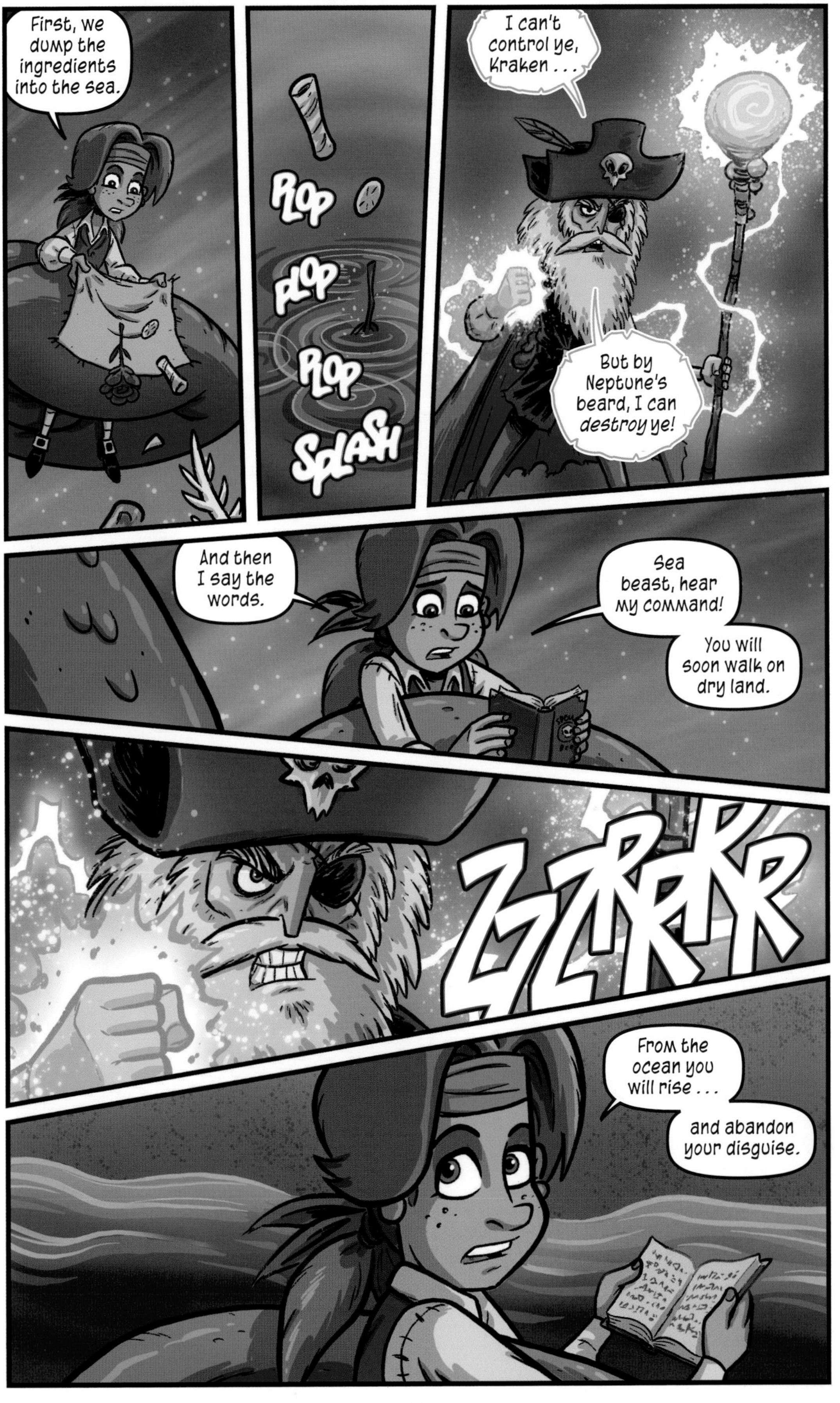
First, we dump the ingredients into the sea.
PLOP
PLOP
PLOP
SPLASH
I can't control ye, Kraken . . .
But by Neptune's beard, I can *destroy* ye!
And then I say the words.
Sea beast, hear my command!
You will soon walk on dry land.
ZZRRRR
From the ocean you will rise . . .
and abandon your disguise.

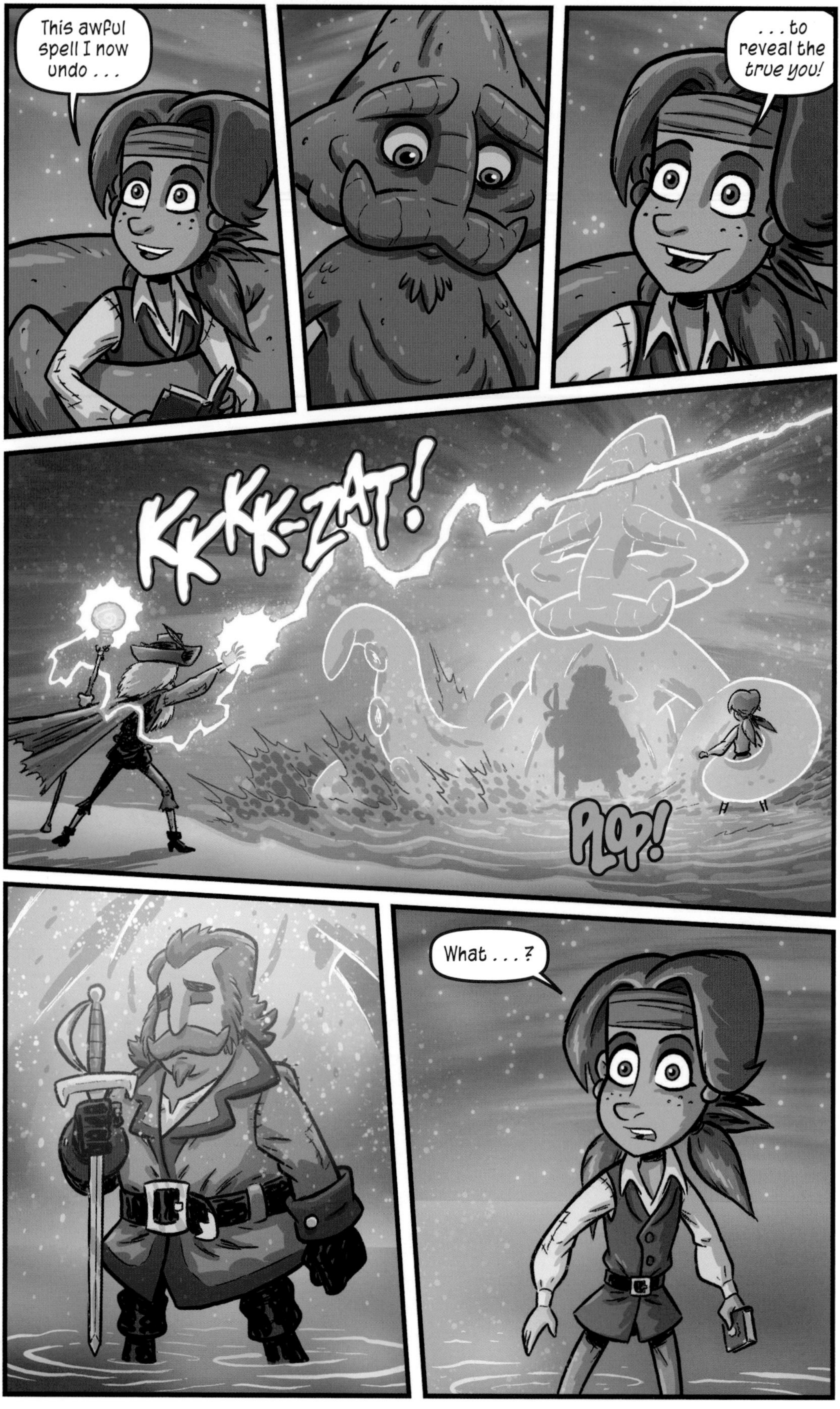
This awful spell I now undo . . .
. . . to reveal the true you!
KKKK-ZAT!
PLOP!
What . . . ?

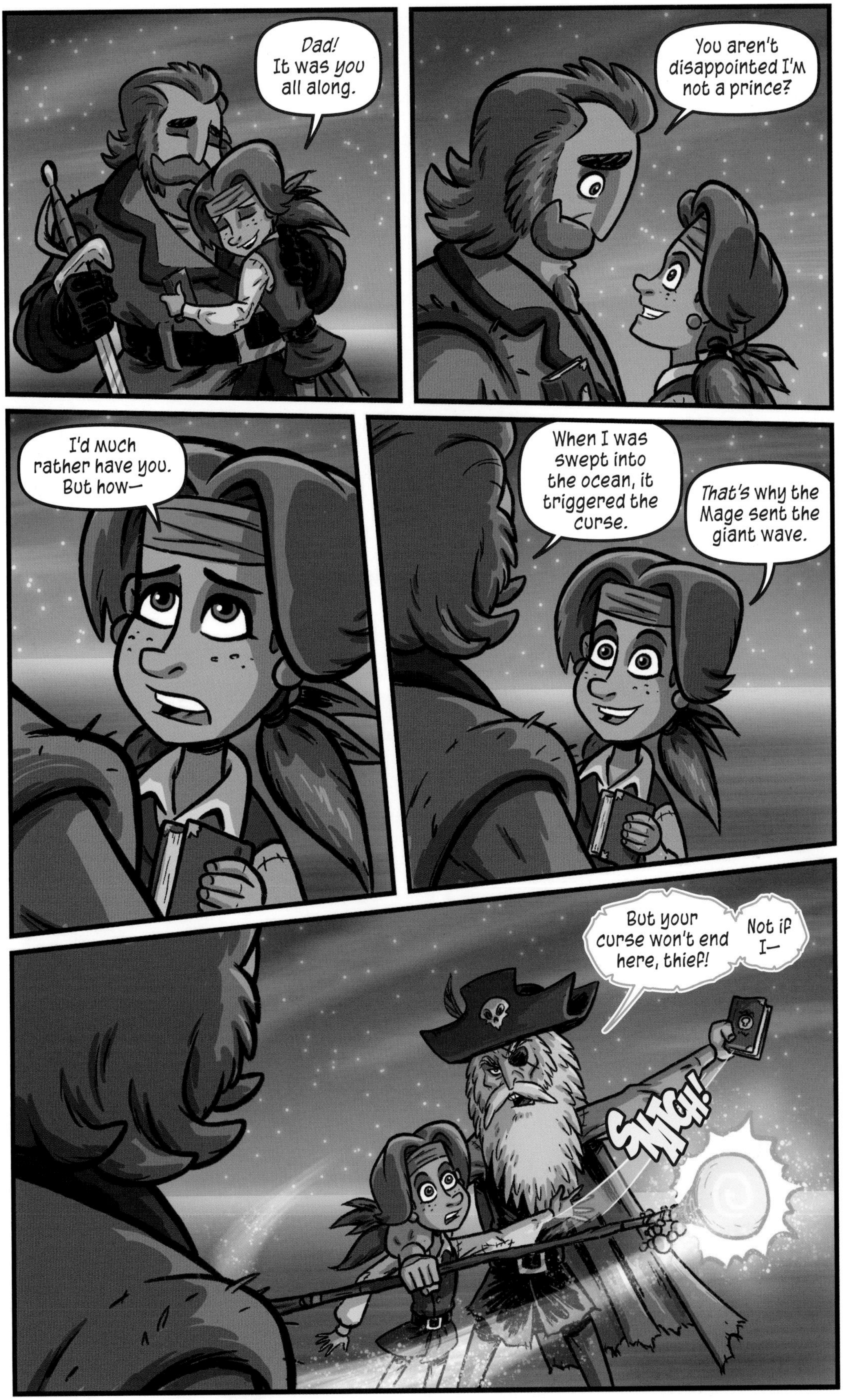
Dad! It was *you* all along.
You aren't disappointed I'M not a prince?
I'd much rather have you. But how—
When I was swept into the ocean, it triggered the curse.
That's why the Mage sent the giant wave.
But your curse won't end here, thief!
Not if I—
SNATCH!

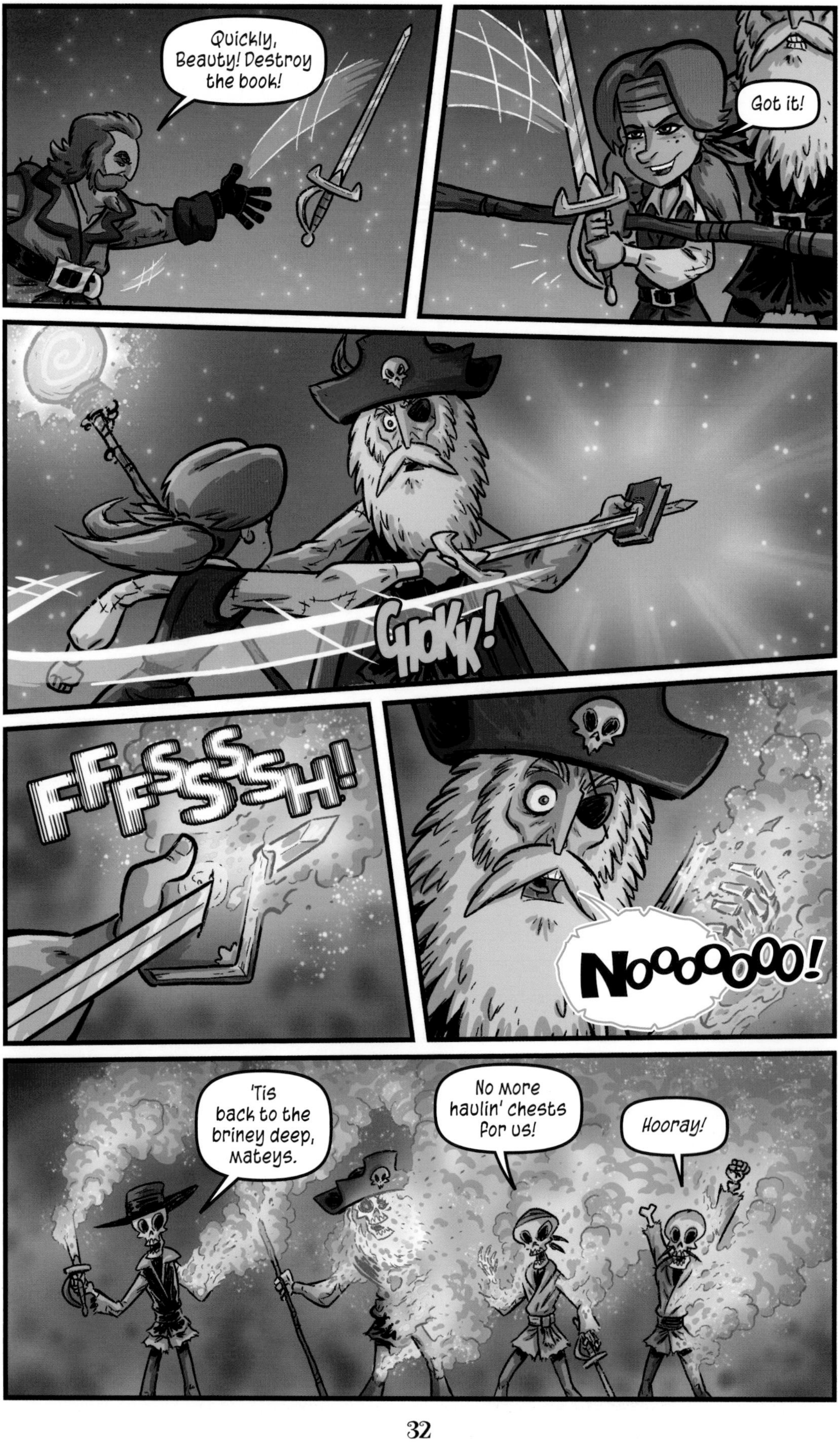

Quickly, Beauty! Destroy the book!
Got it!
CHOKK!
FFFSSSSSH!
Nooooooo!
'Tis back to the briney deep, Mateys.
No more haulin' chests for us!
Hooray!

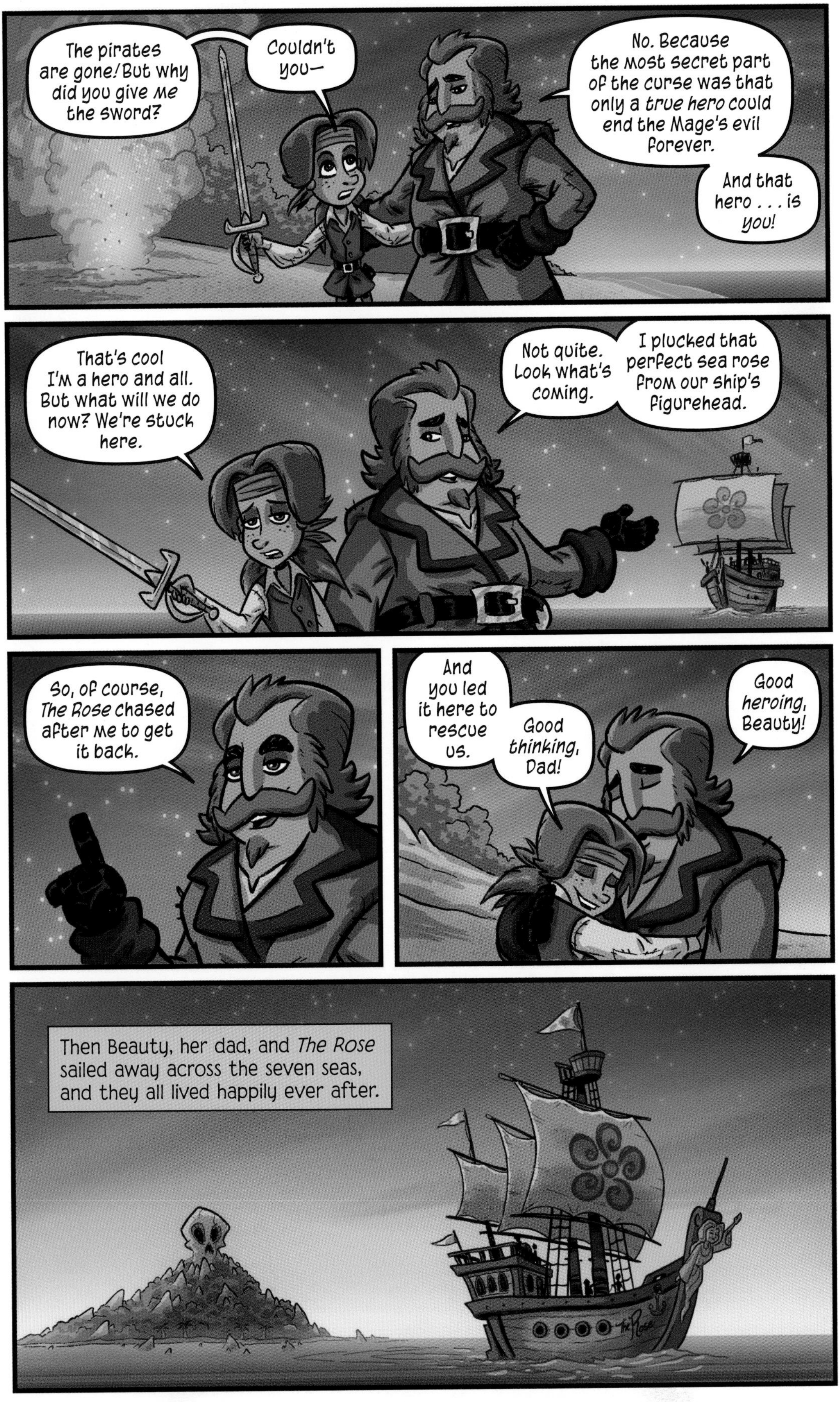
The pirates are gone! But why did you give me the sword?
Couldn't you—
No. Because the most secret part of the curse was that only a *true hero* could end the Mage's evil forever.
And that hero . . . is *you!*
That's cool I'm a hero and all. But what will we do now? We're stuck here.
Not quite. Look what's coming.
I plucked that perfect sea rose from our ship's figurehead.
So, of course, *The Rose* chased after me to get it back.
And you led it here to rescue us.
Good thinking, Dad!
Good *heroing*, Beauty!
Then Beauty, her dad, and *The Rose* sailed away across the seven seas, and they all lived happily ever after.
The Rose

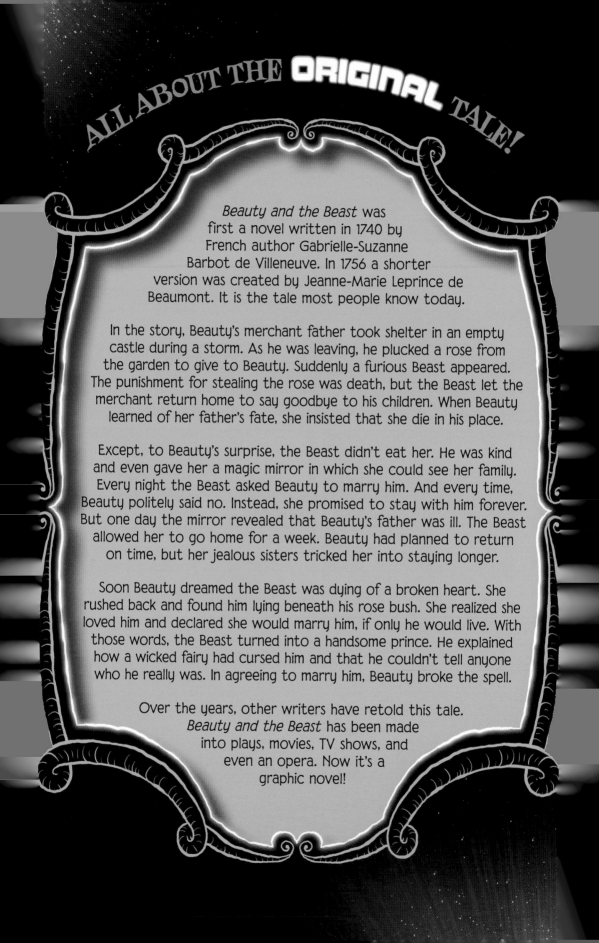

ALL ABOUT THE ORIGINAL TALE!

Beauty and the Beast was first a novel written in 1740 by French author Gabrielle-Suzanne Barbot de Villeneuve. In 1756 a shorter version was created by Jeanne-Marie Leprince de Beaumont. It is the tale most people know today.

In the story, Beauty's merchant father took shelter in an empty castle during a storm. As he was leaving, he plucked a rose from the garden to give to Beauty. Suddenly a furious Beast appeared. The punishment for stealing the rose was death, but the Beast let the merchant return home to say goodbye to his children. When Beauty learned of her father's fate, she insisted that she die in his place.

Except, to Beauty's surprise, the Beast didn't eat her. He was kind and even gave her a magic mirror in which she could see her family. Every night the Beast asked Beauty to marry him. And every time, Beauty politely said no. Instead, she promised to stay with him forever. But one day the mirror revealed that Beauty's father was ill. The Beast allowed her to go home for a week. Beauty had planned to return on time, but her jealous sisters tricked her into staying longer.

Soon Beauty dreamed the Beast was dying of a broken heart. She rushed back and found him lying beneath his rose bush. She realized she loved him and declared she would marry him, if only he would live. With those words, the Beast turned into a handsome prince. He explained how a wicked fairy had cursed him and that he couldn't tell anyone who he really was. In agreeing to marry him, Beauty broke the spell.

Over the years, other writers have retold this tale. *Beauty and the Beast* has been made into plays, movies, TV shows, and even an opera. Now it's a graphic novel!

A FAR OUT GUIDE TO THE TALE'S SEAFARING TWISTS!

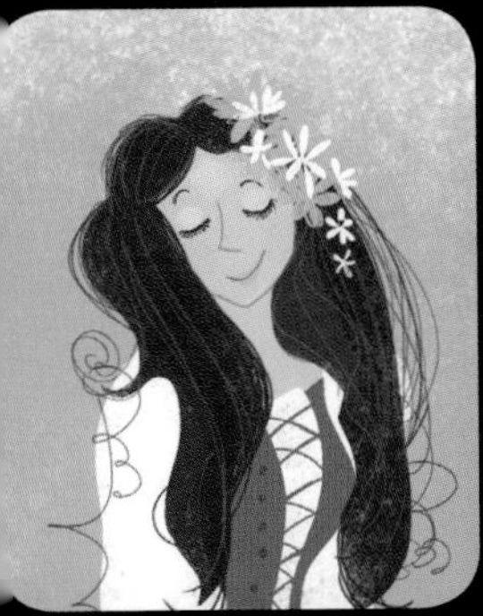

Beauty isn't just the daughter of a merchant. She's a heroic sailor!

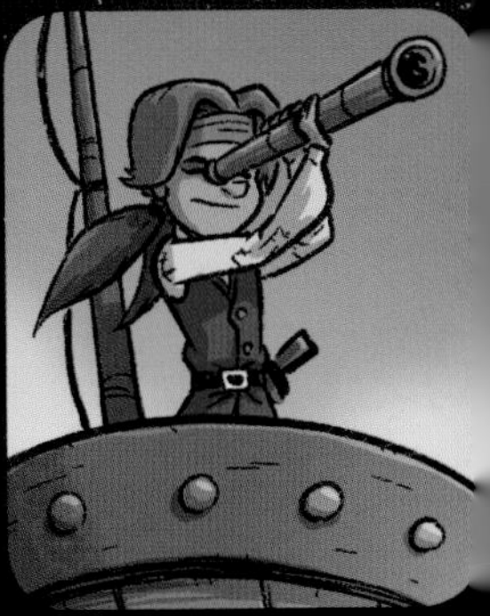

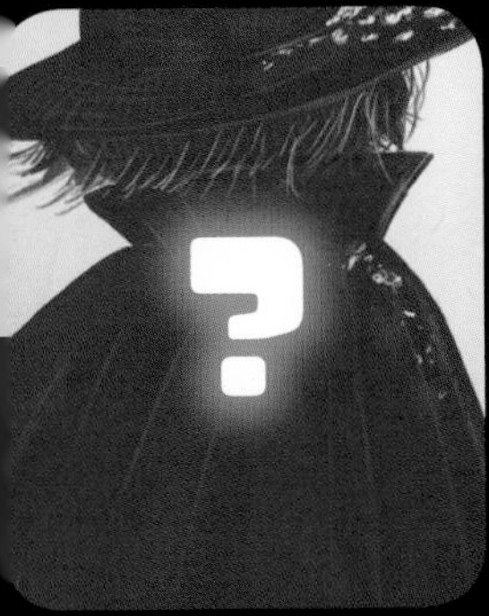

We don't know what the original beast looks like. Here he's a fearsome sea monster.

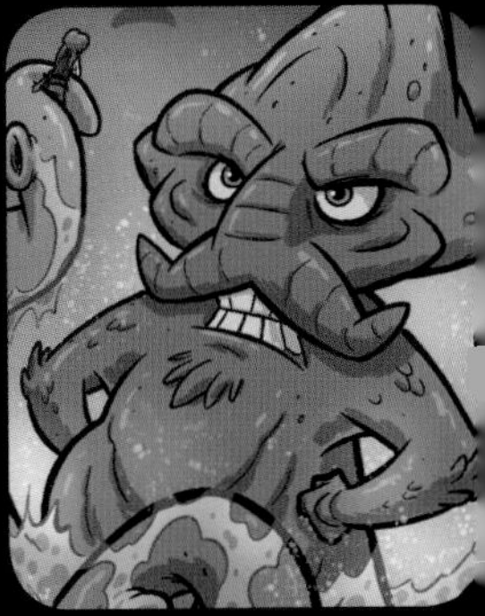

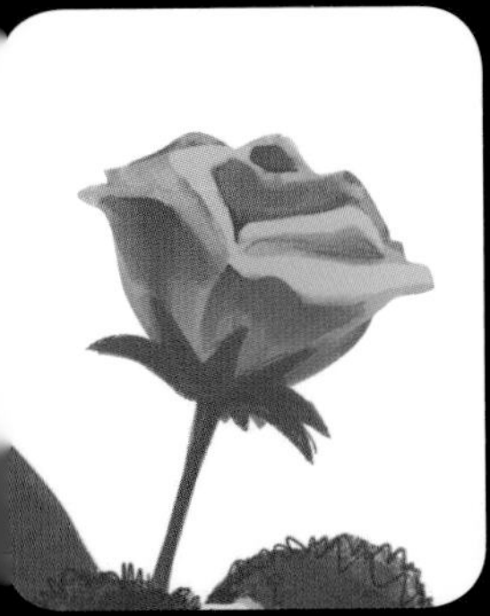

In the original, a stolen rose causes trouble. In this tale, a sea rose helps solve the problem.

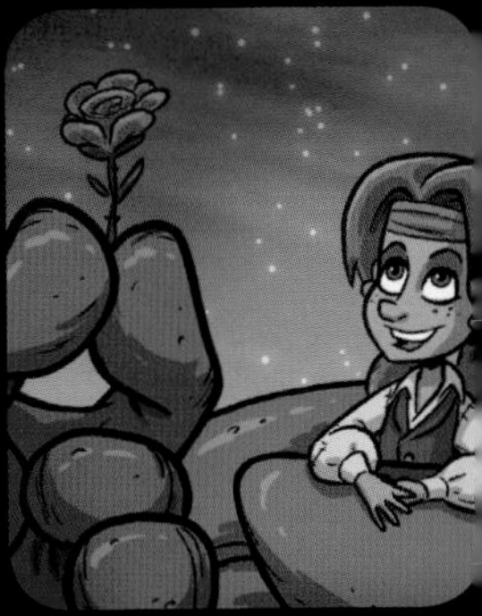

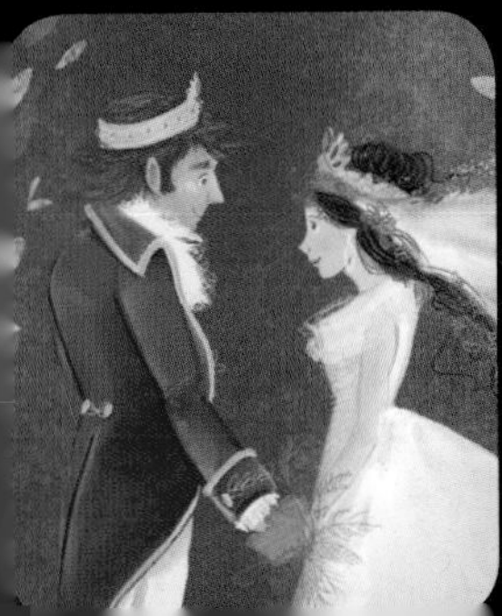

After Beauty breaks the curse, the sea beast doesn't transform into a prince. He becomes Beauty's lost father!

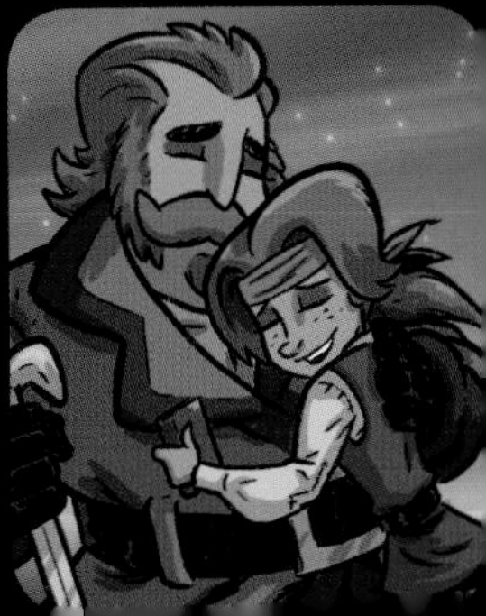

VISUAL QUESTIONS

Describe Beauty's character. How did she change throughout the story? How did she stay the same? Use examples to support your answer.

Do you think it was wise for Beauty to make the bargain with the Kraken? Why or why not? What would you have done?

Were you surprised the Kraken was actually Beauty's dad? Why or why not? Look through the story and find at least two moments that hint at the beast's true identity.

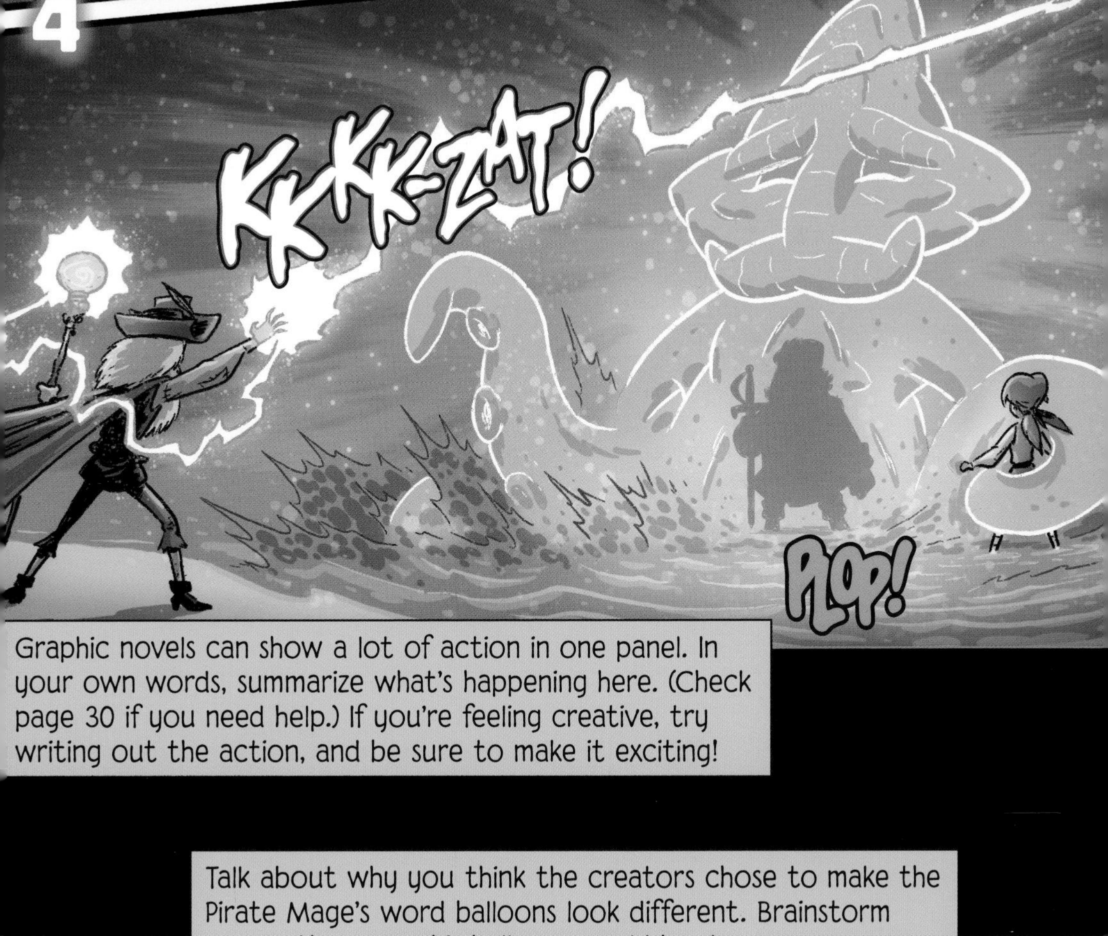
4
KKKK-ZAT!
PLOP!

Graphic novels can show a lot of action in one panel. In your own words, summarize what's happening here. (Check page 30 if you need help.) If you're feeling creative, try writing out the action, and be sure to make it exciting!

Talk about why you think the creators chose to make the Pirate Mage's word balloons look different. Brainstorm some other ways his balloons could be drawn.

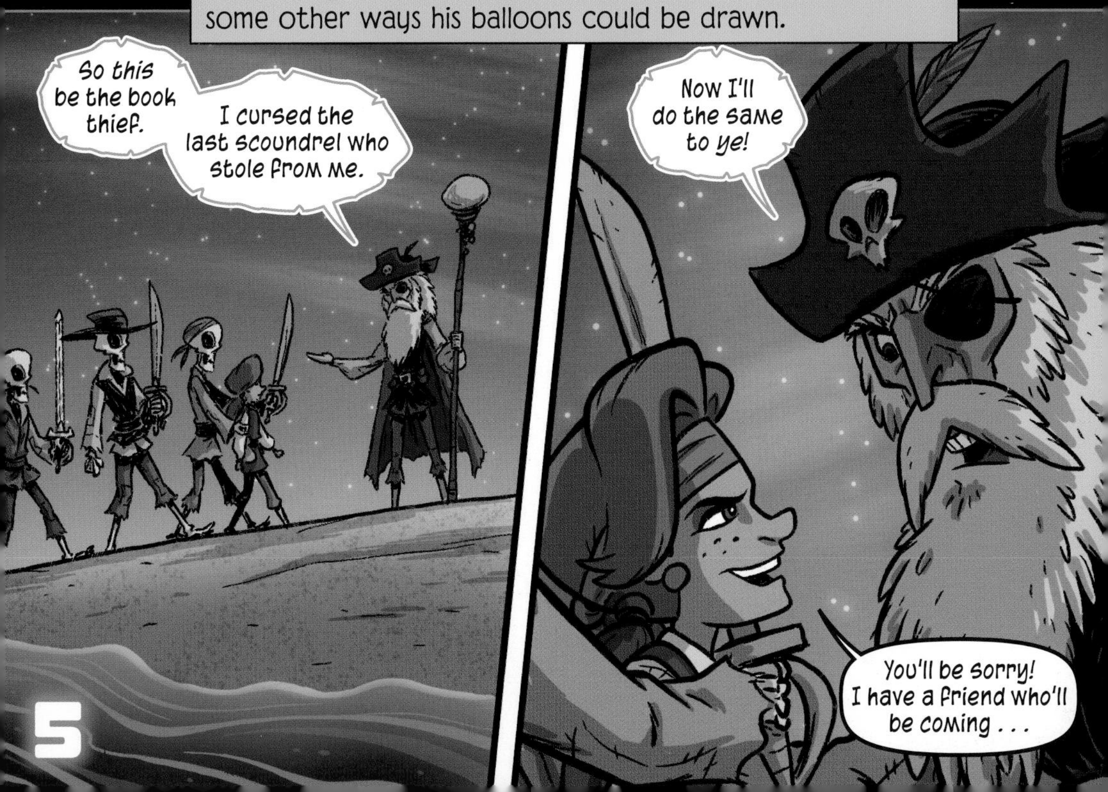
So this be the book thief.
I cursed the last scoundrel who stole from me.
Now I'll do the same to ye!
You'll be sorry! I have a friend who'll be coming . . .
5

AUTHOR

Louise Simonson writes comics and books about monsters, science fiction and fantasy characters, and super heroes. She wrote the award-winning Power Pack series, several best-selling X-Men titles, Web of Spiderman for Marvel Comics, and Superman: The Man of Steel and Steel for DC Comics. She has also written many books for kids. She is married to comic artist and writer Walter Simonson and lives in the suburbs of New York City.

ILLUSTRATOR

Otis Frampton is a comic book writer and illustrator. He is also one of the character and background artists on the popular animated web series How It Should Have Ended. His comic book series Oddly Normal is published by Image Comics.

GLOSSARY

ahoy (uh-HOY)—a call used by sailors to greet passing ships or to get people's attention

bargain (BAHR-guhn)—a deal between people (or a girl and a Kraken) in which they agree to do or give something in order to get something else

curse (KURS)—an evil spell meant to harm someone

dreaded (DRED-ed)—greatly feared

figurehead (FIG-yer-hed)—an image of a person or thing that's been carved into the front of a sailing ship

ingredient (in-GREE-dee-uhnt)—something that is mixed together with other things to create something new

Kraken (KRAH-kuhn)—a huge, legendary sea monster

mage (MAYJ)—a person who uses magic

mainsail (MAYN-sayl)—a large and important sail found behind the main mast, which is a strong, tall pole in the center of a ship

merchant (MUR-chuhnt)—involved in the buying and selling of things to make money; also, a person who buys and sells things to make money

ration (RASH-uhn)—an amount of food given to sailors or soldiers daily

transform (trans-FORM)—to change completely

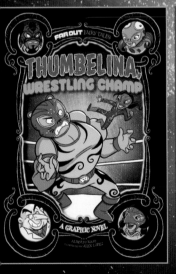